Augustus Mongredien

Frank Allerton

An Autobiography - Vol. 1

Augustus Mongredien

Frank Allerton
An Autobiography - Vol. 1

ISBN/EAN: 9783337123635

Printed in Europe, USA, Canada, Australia, Japan

Cover: Foto ©Raphael Reischuk / pixelio.de

More available books at **www.hansebooks.com**

FRANK ALLERTON:

An Autobiography.

BY

AUGUSTUS MONGREDIEN.

"Non ulla Musis pagina gratior,
Quam quæ severis ludicra jungere
Novit, fatigatamque nugis
Utilibus recreare mentem."

IN THREE VOLUMES.

VOL. I.

London:

SAMUEL TINSLEY & CO.,

10 SOUTHAMPTON STREET, STRAND.

1878.

CONTENTS OF VOL. I.

FRANK ALLERTON:

AN AUTOBIOGRAPHY.

CHAPTER I.

MY ENTRANCE INTO LIFE. 1718.

WHERE is the man, woman, or child that is not fond of a story? In all ages the human race, and at all ages human beings, have taken delight both in historic records, which are often false, and in works of fiction, which are often true. But to me biography is of all forms of narrative the most interesting, especially when the biographer is an autobiographer. In the latter case it is like Rembrandt's portrait, painted by himself. The worker is at once the producer and the subject of the work.

Of all the works of antiquity those that, in my opinion, we could least spare are old Plutarch's Lives and the splendid historical romance of Quintus Curtius. What we want is not a mere chronological record or a dry catalogue of events, but the spirited touches and racy descriptions which give us a clear conception of the men treated of, and impress us with a sense of their life and reality. We all like to observe the different ways in which different people have been affected by the same circumstances, to trace the motives by which each has been actuated, and to compare the impressions which a given train of events did produce on them and would have produced on ourselves.

Such is the infinite variety of human character, that its combinations are inexhaustible, and our curiosity is never sated. Indeed, our pleasure is not only enhanced by, but chiefly derived from, that wonderful diversity. Every human being has his own peculiar mental and moral features, just as his face has its own special physiognomy, which (Dromios apart) can never be mistaken for another. Nor has any human life ever been the exact counterpart of any other life. This divergence runs through the whole of our habits and modes of being. Fifty children at school are taught by one writing-master, and their elementary pot-hooks and hangers exhibit a great family likeness; but as they progress, individuality asserts itself, and finally no two handwritings are alike. Straightforward, clear-headed men write a crabbed and illegible scrawl, while dull drivellers frequently clothe their nonsense in fine, bold, clear characters. In the sexes this distinctiveness is signally evinced. With rare exceptions, the difference between the handwriting of a man and that of a woman is so marked that one can scarcely ever be taken for the other.

Let these remarks be my apology for writing the story of the most eventful period of my life. No one is a good judge of his own performances; but I fancy that if I read these adventures as having happened to a stranger, I should not find them altogether devoid of interest.

I was born in 1718, at Paris, where my father, Andrew Allerton, then resided. Ours is an old Berkshire family, and the estate at Allerton, with its mansion, the Allerton Manor House, had been in the possession of the family for untold generations; but it was then so deeply mortgaged that the rents did little more than cover the interest. For that and for some other reasons my father resided abroad. As for my mother, I never knew her, as she had died in giving me birth.

I shall skim very lightly at present over my father's history, as more ample details will hereafter be given in connexion with some stirring incidents in my own life. It will be sufficient now to state that, when I was five years of age, my father brought me over to England, and left me in the charge and under the guardianship of my uncle and aunt, Mr. and Mrs. Uppenham. To my uncle he assigned the management and stewardship of the Allerton estate, and any surplus, after paying the interest on the mortgages, was to be used to defray the expense of my maintenance and education. My father then returned to Paris, where he died a year or two afterwards.

Mr. Meredith Uppenham had married a sister of my father's, and they had one child, a daughter, named Alice. She was a joyous, little toddling thing, with long flaxen curly hair, two or three years younger than myself, who was as delighted to have a playmate as I was, so that we soon became fast friends.

My uncle's character will sufficiently develope itself in the sequel to obviate the necessity of my saying more at present than that he was a most estimable and kind-hearted man, exceedingly well informed, and always adding to his stock of information by constant reading. Without being wealthy, his means were more than adequate to his wants, and he lived a life of learned leisure.

Mrs. Uppenham, my aunt, was a woman of handsome features, commanding presence, and of considerable intellectual power. Whatever she felt and willed, she felt and willed strongly. She was staunch in her beliefs and affections, inflexible in her resolutions, and almost painfully conscientious in the performance of what she deemed her duty. She was deeply attached to my lovable uncle, over whom she at the same time exercised great influence.

From early associations as well as from family traditions, both were warm adherents of the Jacobite cause, and their sincere fealty to the Protestant Church did not interfere with their ardent zeal for the restoration of the Catholic dynasty of the Stuarts.

Such was the family of which I was admitted a member, at so early a period in my life that I never had any but the vaguest and dreamiest recollections of any other home. In every respect I was treated as a beloved son; and little Alice and I played together, studied together, and glided away from childhood together in the free intimacy of brother and sister.

My aunt had, from some reason or other, imbibed a rooted dislike to public schools, and, having inoculated her husband with the same prejudice, it was determined that the two children should receive the unalloyed benefit of home education. Our early years were therefore subjected to the training at first of a governess only, then of a governess backed and reinforced by masters, and at last of masters only.

By the time that I was fourteen years of age, I had really learned a good deal; but it was evident to my uncle that there were some other elements, indispensable to complete the education of a man, which I had still to acquire, and which I never should acquire under my present system of instruction. It was not that manly exercises had been neglected: in fencing, riding, rowing, swimming, &c., I had been well taught, and I was no mean proficient. But a boy is an incomplete boy without a fair amount of male companionship. He is in danger of becoming either a milksop or a prig, unless he comes into contact with the pugnacity, the selfishness, the rivalry, and the petulance of other boys. He requires, on the one hand, to be stirred into emulation, and on the other to be hustled out of undue conceit of his own merits: in the process his sense of self-importance gets weakened, and he gradually settles down to his proper level. Such experiences are very necessary to a lad to prepare him for his entrance into the world, where, if some degree of self-knowledge has not previously been attained, it is only to be acquired at an exorbitantly high price.

After some discussion, during which there was an upheaval of that deep-lying stratum of firmness in my uncle's mind which rarely came to the surface, but to which, when it did, my aunt always discreetly succumbed, it was settled that I was to be sent to some finishing-school, where I might consort with lads of my own age, or older.

"And now, my dear Meredith," said my aunt, "that I have yielded to your wishes (and I promise to faithfully carry them out), you must leave to me the selection of the school to which Frank is to be sent. It must be none of your seminaries for Whiggism, your Hanoverian conscience-traps, your hot-beds for disloyalty and infidelity, but a reputable institution, conducted by some pious, learned, and old-fashioned Episcopalian, free from the leaven of revolutionary principles, and equally free from the taint of papistical tendencies."

"Very good, my dear," said my uncle; "I leave it to you, but with one proviso: it must be a large school. I want Frank to be thrown among a crowd of his fellows, to feel the jostling and pressure of the throng; I want him to know by experience something of the bad as well as of the good of this world; I want him to have his temper tried, his wishes thwarted, his kindness abused, his credulity laughed at, and, generally, his toes trodden on. All this cannot be effectually accomplished at a small school. A hundred boys is my *minimum*. Please to remember that this is my *sine quâ non*."

My aunt acquiesced, and set to work to find an establishment that should combine her husband's and her own requirements. After many inquiries and advertisements, both answered and inserted, my aunt fixed on Dr. Burridge's Academy at Highgate, as fulfilling all the *desiderata*, and, after some correspondence with the doctor, which she deemed satisfactory, and consultation with two friends who shared her political views, and whose sons were committed to his care, I was entered as a pupil in Dr. Burridge's establishment.

CHAPTER II.

I GO TO SCHOOL.   1732—1735.

On the resumption of studies after the mid-summer holidays my uncle escorted me to Virgil House, and formally consigned me into the charge of Dr. Burridge.

Virgil House was, as it were, twins, two mansions in the Grove at Highgate having been thrown into one. It was a very large establishment, and, being both expensive and fashionable, the pupils were generally the sons of persons in good position. But my aunt was quite mistaken in the notion she had formed that the inculcation of Tory principles went hand in hand with Greek and Latin in the educational scheme of Dr. Burridge. Half the pupils, at least, were the scions of Whig families, who were under the contrary impression that Whig doctrines were there instilled along with grammar and mathematics. But Dr. Burridge steered clear both of the Tory Scylla and the Whig Charybdis. He contented himself with giving his pupils a thoroughly sound education, totally irrespective of political controversies; and thus my aunt, like a true woman, had selected the right school for the wrong reasons.

Tall, portly, and dignified, with a face resting on massive, square jaw-bones, and arched over by huge, shaggy eyebrows, Dr. Burridge was evidently a man not to be trifled with; but there was a benevolent and almost a merry twinkle in his deep-seated but sharp grey eyes, of which the attractiveness neutralized the awe which his sterner physical attributes created. While he was indifferent to, and perhaps entertained a kind of philosophical disdain for, both extremes of political partisanship, he so ingeniously coquetted with those cautious parents who, before entrusting him with their precious offspring, were desirous of ascertaining his own private views on politics, that, whichever side they were upon, they generally went away with the impression that the Doctor, while too discreet to commit himself, was "all right."

And thus it occurred that his school was attended by boys whose parents represented every shade of political opinion.

Dr. Burridge so overflowed with learning that it ran over the brim and spilt all round him. It oozed out of him in the shape of classical quotations—long Latinized words ending in *ible, ity,* and *ation*—and sententious remarks as dogmatic, and sometimes as ambiguous, as the oracle of Delphi.

This flow of erudition fascinated the parents, who thought that by living in such an atmosphere of learning their sons must surely imbibe some of it; and, in conjunction with a deep, sonorous voice, a burly form, and the alternate rise and depression of those vast shaggy eyebrows, it awed the boys into wondering submissiveness.

" My dear Dr. Burridge," said my uncle, after having introduced me, " I am sure, from what I have heard of you, and from what you have written to Mrs. Uppenham, that you will take care to foster in my nephew those sound principles as to Church and State which will conduce to his well-being in after life."

"Worthy sir," replied Dr. Burridge, with the emphasis which underscored his slightest sayings, "principles are the groundwork of character. If the foundation be sound, the superstructure is secure. *Testa semel imbuta*, &c."

"You may perhaps know, indeed may perhaps share, the opinion which I hold as to the indefeasible rights of a legitimate king. I feel that I am safe in talking of these matters with you."

"You are. I am the inviolate depository of many similar confidences. The struggles between abstract right and expediency are not unknown to me."

"I see you take my meaning."

"I do. It is the old encounter between *de jure* and *de facto*. Heaven will protect the right."

"Amen !—Dr. Burridge, I see that you are one of the right sort. I commend Frank to your kind care. Adieu ! "

And my uncle departed, charmed with the orthodoxy of the Doctor's opinions, although to what they really were he had carefully abstained from giving any clue.

After undergoing the ordeal of mystifications and persecutions to which the " new boy " is always subject, I soon got initiated, and settled down resignedly, if not cheerfully, to my work. In a short time I had formed a special attachment to one of my schoolfellows, a bright, merry boy of about my own age, named Charles Frampton; and he took a similar fancy to me. We helped each other in our lessons, we shared each other's treats, and we fought each other's battles. We became inseparable, and constantly strolled together with our arms round each other's necks, making all manner of mutual confidences and confessions. To my surprise, I discovered that he was a full-blown Hanoverian Whig. For the moment I was quite shocked. I had been taught at home to consider the supporters of the intrusive dynasty as mean time-servers, who abandoned their rightful sovereign in distress, and curried favour with the usurper from low and mercenary motives. But, as I had no strong personal feeling in the matter, I soon recovered, and said to Charley,—

" I had no idea that you were a common Brunswick man. I am for the rightful king, I am. But never mind; I like you, Charley, and I 'll look that over."

" And I," said Charley, " will wink at your being a silly old Jacobite. After all, who cares? Shall we have a game at leap-frog ? "

" Stop, Charley! This is what puzzles me. How did you manage to get into this school ? The Doctor, you know, is an out-and-out ' King and his rights' man, and would no more let a Whig in than a——" Here I was hard up for a simile—" an elephant."

" You gumph! Why it 's just the contrary. He is dead for the Protestant succession."

" Nonsense; you don't say so ? "

" At least, he led my mother to believe so. My mother brought me here, you know. She and the Doctor talked a lot, and here is what they said."

From what he told me, I make out that what passed must have been something like the following. I shall not record every one of the learned quotations with which Dr. Burridge interlarded his discourse; they would be unintelligible to many, and savour of pedantry to all; nor would they serve any purpose, as he used them not to express, but simply to illustrate, his meaning. I may take this opportunity of stating that, for somewhat similar reasons, I have, throughout this work, omitted the cursing and swearing, the silly oaths and foul words, which are of such common use (though perhaps less now than some years ago) among all classes of men. With rare exceptions, they are mere thoughtless, unmeaning expletives, the outcome of habit and routine, that neither add force to language nor serve for the delineation of character. They are disgusting both to write and to read, and I will not sully my pages with them. While I am about it, I may add that, when I introduce a foreigner speaking English, it shall not be in the imperfect language which he really uses. An exact transcript of it, when thoroughly carried out, produces a jargon which is sometimes unintelligible and always tiresome, and, when carried out partially, is much more unnatural than when not attempted at all; for that a person should speak partly in broken and partly in pure English is a perpetual and perplexing violation of reality. My object is, more to convey the meaning of the speaker than to set down his actual words, except in those cases in which his mode of expression is as essential a characteristic as are his thoughts themselves.

On the occasion of bringing Charley to Virgil House, Mrs. Frampton, whom he somewhat irreverently described as being in the habit of chopping up her sentences into small mouthfuls, to enable them, as he said, to go down more easily, spoke thus,—

" Dr. Burridge, listen, please. Lady Griggs, —you know Lady Griggs ? "

" Madam, Lady Griggs is the revered consort of my revered friend, Alderman Sir Jeremiah Griggs."

" She recommended me here. ' Dr. Burridge,' says she, ' is staunch; send Charley to him.' ' Staunch in what ? ' says I. ' Glorious revolution,' says she. Are you that ? "

" Madam, all revolutions are glorious when they tend to improvement. Time, madam, —*tempus edax rerum,*—rolls heavily over and crushes into extinction old, worm-eaten, and effete institutions. If new ones spring up, better suited to the requirements of the age, let us hail them!"

"Beautifully put, Doctor! Then Lady Griggs—a very great friend of mine, you know—told me, 'You will find the Doctor,' says she, 'strong, amazingly strong, on Protestant succession.'"

"Madam, I am strong on all matters tending to the welfare of our beloved country. Those conditions which are essential to it I not only readily conform to, but cheerfully accept, and, as long as they last, will strenuously contend for."

"Dear me! how fine! My husband, Mr. Frampton,—you know Mr. Frampton, of the Secret Service Office,—well, 'I hear,' says he, 'that the Doctor is right.' 'About what?' says I. 'Whig principles,' says he. Are you?"

"Madam, if I may define Whigs as the champions of progress, and their opponents as the advocates of immutability, who can hesitate between them?"

"Well, I do admire that in you, Doctor. You don't just say, 'Yes' or 'No' to my questions—that is what ordinary people do—but you give reasons, and then I know where I am. ' Ask the Doctor,' says my husband, ' which he is for.' ' What is which ? ' says I. ' Moving on or going back ? ' says he. What shall I tell him, Doctor ? "

" Tell him, madam,.that all changes for the better are acceptable to me. *Tempora mutantur*, and so must everything else. What we want is improvement : improvement implies change : *ergo*, those who resist change, resist improvement. *Q. E. D.*"

" Nothing can be more explicit. Your frankness delights me : I am perfectly satisfied. Take great care of Charles. Adieu ! "

When I told Charlie of the corresponding scene, when I had been introduced to the Doctor by my father, we were much amused by the contrast. But, boy-like, thinking very little of the sanctity of convictions, we voted Dr. Burridge to have been by far the cleverest actor in those little interludes.

The school was a large and well-conducted one. We had a good supply of clever instructors ; and yet the strain on the pupils was not made too heavy. In extreme cases Dr. Burridge was a strict disciplinarian, and flog-

ging was mercilessly resorted to. But to
those breaches of school-law that arose from a
sluggish intellect, or that sprang out of high
spirits or sudden impulse, he was lenient in
corporal punishment, although ruthless in the
infliction of magniloquent expostulation ; indeed, we would sometimes have preferred a
mild birching to a prolonged remonstrance.
But, at all events, he drew a line,—he did not
preach and flog too ; and, on the whole, we all
of us liked and respected the Doctor.

As to influence over our religious or political
opinions, he never tried to exercise any. He
neither uprooted our old tenets nor inculcated
fresh. His pupils never could discover whether
he were Whig or Tory, High Church or Low
Church. In regard to such topics, he was a
mere " chip in porridge," which, after all, is a
much better thing than " death in the pot."

On the other hand, he never let slip an
opportunity of exalting and glorifying to us
the higher virtues, such as truthfulness; self-
respect, generosity, and brotherly love ; and, in
consequence, a healthy feeling and a manly
tone pervaded the school. It was quite stirring
to hear the large-hearted pedant earnestly

preaching peace and good-will in defiant, trumpet-like tones, and proclaiming, with the voice of a Stentor and the emphasis of a Demosthenes, his favourite saying, that union with others you cannot enforce, but charity to others you can always practise.

I spent three happy and not unprofitable years at Virgil House. About once a month I walked to my uncle's on the Saturday afternoon, and returned to Highgate early on the Monday morning; so that, with these occasional, in addition to the usual Midsummer holidays, my intercourse with my adopted home in Red Lion Square and its kind inmates was not severed by any long break.

That dear old village, Highgate, where our school was situated, is a very small place, a few miles from London, and was so called from the toll-gate in its centre, that stands on the high road from London to the North. It consists of a few mansions, a few shops, and a disproportionate number of inns and taverns, of which the chief and oldest is the old Gate House. It is at this inn chiefly, but also in smaller number at the Rose and Crown, the Angel, and the Flask, that the absurd but

ancient practice of swearing on the Horns, as
it is called, is forced on most of those travellers
who have not the courage to resist or the means
of buying off the infliction. Many from weakness, some from curiosity, and not a few for
the fun of the thing, acquiesce in the grotesque
ceremony, and, as I and Charley more than
once witnessed, made fools of themselves for
the amusement of clowns and the profit of inn-
keepers. The landlord of the Gate House told
us, "There is so much doing in this way that
I am obliged to hire a man as swearer-in. I
have sworn in from a hundred to a hundred
and twenty in a day. Bodies of tailors come
up here from town, bringing five or six new
shopmates with them to be sworn; and I often
have parties of ladies and gentlemen in private
carriages come up purposely to be made free
of Highgate in this way." The mere swearing in is not a long or difficult affair; but it
results in a large expenditure for beer or wine
on the part of the victim, drunkenness on the
part of the sharers of the feast, and the pocket-
ing of a heavy score on the part of the landlord.

Ever since my school-boy days I have re-

tained an affectionate recollection of old Highgate, with its elevated position and its magni-
ficent views of London. The two ponds near
the Gate House were formed by the excavation
of gravel which was taken to make the low
road in Holloway. Old Fuller, alluding to this
removal of the soil from one place to the other,
calls it " a two-handed charity, providing water
on the hill, where it was wanted, and cleanli-
ness in the valley, which before was passed
with difficulty."

CHAPTER III.

CHEVALIER DE LIVORDY.   1735—1736.

AFTER leaving school I continued my studies at home under the direction of my uncle, and with the assistance of various masters. My uncle was an excellent classical scholar, and a glutton at reading books of all sorts. It was, however, the old Latin commentators and emendators, Scaliger, Vossius, Salmasius, and others, that he chiefly delighted in. He loved to poke into the holes and corners of literature, and to drag out of those neglected recesses some piece of ingenious criticism, or spicy paradox, or biographical scandal. He would now and then pick out some forgotten writer, some faded celebrity, such as Postellus or Trithemius, and descant upon his eccentric teachings; or he would fish up from the depths of

oblivion some unread Latin poet, such as
Audoenus or Vida, and declaim against the injustice and caprice of popular applause. He
would say, "You talk of the dryness of my
studies! Nonsense! You do not know the
fun there is in those old fellows. Why, who
can read Plato's 'Hippias Major' without a
hearty laugh? There is not a comic scene in
Molière that is so amusing. Again, read the
letters that passed between Politian and his
friend Barbarus about the gender of the word
'culex.' The correspondence commences on
both sides by the most fulsome compliments
and expressions of intense esteem and admiration. Gradually, as the dispute warms, the
regard cools; and at about the twelfth exchange
of letters they wind up by blackguarding each
other furiously, and all about the doubtful
gender of the word 'culex'! Then look at
the cruel fate of Peter l'Ach! You smile?
Just the way of the world! You laugh at a
name which you ought to revere. Denmark
ought to be as proud of Petrus Pachius *poeta*
as of Tycho Brahe. He was the greatest Latin
poet since Virgil. He wrote, among other
ingenious works, the 'Pugna Porcorum,' a

poem of 1,000 hexameters, every word in which literally began with the letter *p*. Match me that if you can. Now, again, you ladies pique yourselves on your knowledge of music and musical composers. Very well. There is a composition of world-wide celebrity, that attracts crowded and appreciative auditories, and is never listened to but with intense admiration. Nor is it a mere cantata, but a lengthened performance. I allude to the splendid 'Miserere,' which is chanted every Good Friday at the Sistine Chapel in Rome. It is confessedly the work of a composer of the very highest order of merit. Do you know his name? No? Of course not. You very likely have never heard of it. It is Tommaso Baj! Another instance of capricious injustice in the distribution of fame." But it was only when among ourselves that my uncle indulged in this vein. In general society he was, like Addison, reticent, kept his learning within bounds, and rarely made a quotation.

I found my old playmate, cousin Alice, just hovering on the confines between girlhood and womanhood. A dainty age, that sweet fifteen, when, day by day, figure, face, and mind develope fresh charms, and gradually grow and expand into their perfect forms. Among her many accomplishments, music held a high place. She was passionately fond of it, and her exquisite performance on the harpsichord was only surpassed by the sweet, thrilling, and sympathetic tones of her voice when singing. I taught her chess, and she taught me to hum a second in a vocal duet; and so passed we our time together as happy as little birds.

My aunt was addicted to theological studies and embroidery. Hooker's 'Polity,' or a volume of quaint, pithy, poetical Jeremy Taylor, reclined on a stand before her, while she worked away like a Penelope at her colour-weaving. Her strength of mind and decision of character carried all the greater weight with us all, because they were never displayed except in affairs of some importance. In ordinary everyday matters she was indulgent and genial to an extent that might induce a careless observer to fancy that she never had her own way; but in reality it was quite the contrary. She reserved her influence for fitting conjunctures, and, when she did speak seriously and express an earnest opinion, she

was listened to with the utmost attention and
deference.   Some have a knack of wearing out
their authority by bringing it forward on every
petty occasion, and it thus gets wasted and
frittered away, grain by grain, on a pack of
trumpery, trivial subjects.

About this time I took fencing lessons from
a celebrated *professeur d'escrime*, the Chevalier
de Livordy.   He was a tall, spare man, of
about fifty, well versed in his art, and wonder-
fully spry and active for his age.   At his
"court," as he called it, which was a spacious
room in St. Martin's Lane, hung round with
weapons of prodigious variety, as well as with
masks, gloves, and defensive armour of all
kinds, I met with many persons of note, for
he was much in vogue.

I learned much from him, and he sometimes
complimented me on my proficiency in the use
of the rapier.   He always dressed well, and,
notwithstanding many peculiarities, had the
address and manners of a gentleman.   His
conversation interested me, and I occasionally
—with the permission of my aunt, which fully
implied that of my uncle—invited him to spend
the evening at our house.

I will give you a sketch of some of the conversations on these occasions, as they may
divert you as they did me. But first I must
tell you something of his history and character.
He professed to be a Frenchman ; but as to his
nationality I have my doubts. He spoke
English so fluently, though with a provincial
accent, and French so indifferently, though
very fond of introducing French phrases, that
his residence of twenty years in London, which
is the period he assigned to it, hardly suffices
to account for his acquiring so much of the
former and forgetting so much of the latter.
Indeed, various little mannerisms have sometimes induced me to think that Ireland must
have been his native country.

He was much addicted to boasting, and in
all matters connected with himself was the
most audacious perverter of truth that I ever
met with. With a soft smile, and a low and
gentle voice, he would utter the most pre-
posterous and startling untruths in relation to
his own doings. His hearers might be deceived for some few minutes, but they soon
detected his exaggerations ; for his statements
were not only incredible, but often contradic-

tory. He did not show any consciousness of the incredulity they excited, but, calm and impassive, he went on from one improbable narrative to another, as coolly as if he had been uttering so many truisms. He saw you lift your eyebrows, but ascribed it to admiration. If his hearers smiled and looked at each other wonderingly, he assumed, or affected to assume, these to be marks of interest.

But, on the other hand, in narrating events, or describing scenes, in which he did not himself figure as an actor, this tendency to distort or exaggerate ceased to appear. He might perhaps embellish, but his imagination never led him in these cases beyond the bounds of probability. He had seen much of the world, and teemed with anecdotes about old customs, past events, and defunct celebrities. As a chronicler he was delightful: it was only when he dealt with his own adventures that he betrayed his weakness, and fell into absurdities. His gentle manners and deferential courtesy to ladies won my aunt's and Alice's favour, and his peculiarities rather amused than offended them.

After the usual general topics had been used

up, such as health and weather, the conversation would direct itself on the particular news of the day.

MR. UPPENHAM. "What a curious story each of the 135 individuals who dined together to-day at Ironmongers' Hall would have to tell!"

MRS. UPPENHAM. "Who were they?"

MR. U. "Men who had from time to time been taken by the Barbary pirates and reduced to slavery. They have been released from captivity by a newly made treaty with the Dey of Algiers."

ALICE. "Were they all Englishmen?"

MR. U. "All; and among them were nine commanders of vessels which had been piratically seized by those wretches."

MRS. U. "The man who is at present King ought to be ashamed of himself to let his subjects be kidnapped in this way, and then meanly beg them off by treaties with this pirate!"

MR. U. "Better that than leave them to their fate. They were presented this morning to George II., who gave them 100*l.*; and many others added donations of five and ten guineas. Sir Charles Wager subscribed 50*l.*"

De Livordy. "Besides, madam, you must bear in mind that this is no new thing. About twenty years ago, the Emperor of Morocco released by treaty 280 Englishmen who had for years been captives in the Moorish states. I saw them go in procession, clad in the Moorish habit, to St. Paul's, where the chaplain of the Bishop of London preached a sermon appropriate to the occasion. After the sermon they proceeded to St. James's, where the King visited them in the garden, and presented them with 500*l.* After this they filed off to Leicester House, and received 250*l.* from the Prince of Wales."

A. "How delighted the families of these men must have been to regain their husbands, or fathers, or brothers, whom they must have given up as lost to them for ever!"

De L. "Not in every case. One of the men I became acquainted with. He had been captured nine years before his deliverance, when mate in a Levant trader. During that time, he was successively quarryman, gardener, cook, and pipe-bearer to an old dervish or priest, who did not treat him very badly. On his return to England, he proceeded to Yarmouth, where he had left his wife and two children. He found, to his dismay, that she had re-married, and was now the mother of three children more. In vain he recalled himself to her recollection; she swore that he was an impostor, and that she had never seen him before in her life. He was so disgusted and disheartened that he went to sea again, and was never heard of more; probably he found his way back to his old master, the dervish."

I. "Besides, in many cases no doubt death must have been busy among the men's families, and poverty have desolated many a hearth."

DE L. "I was myself once very nearly captured by an Algerian corsair. It was a few years before I came over to England that I and three friends engaged a small félouque at Marseilles, for a pleasure trip to Corsica. When about twenty miles from Bastia, a piratical sloop, carrying enormous sails, bore down upon us, and, as escape seemed impos-sible, we determined to make the best resist-ance we could. It was a desperate resolve, as we were only eight, viz., four passengers and four sailors, so that I had to supplement force by stratagem. It happened that we had brought with us four Turkish dresses, with a view to masquerading in Bastia, for it was Carnival time.

" I made my three friends hastily darken their faces and put on the Turkish dresses; and I did the same. I then tied the hands of the four sailors with ropes, and made them lie down, while we, with pistols in hand, stood guard over them. By the time the sloop came alongside of us, we had just completed these preparations. They hailed us, and I replied with a shout, making a salaam. The Algerian captain, seeing us arrayed in orthodox garments, accosted us in language of which I of course did not understand one word. I answered in improvised gibberish, of which he, of course, understood just as little.

" This kind of intercourse could naturally lead to no very satisfactory result; but my calm demeanour (for I listened and spoke with folded arms, and the dignified phlegm of a true Ottoman) completely threw the Algerian off his guard, and he was puzzled to make us out. At last he made up his mind to see with his eyes, since he could not hear with his ears;

and he jumped from the deck of the sloop on
to that of our félouque. He was a big burly
fellow, with a thick grizzled beard, and
squinted so horribly that his eyes seemed as
though one were looking at the other. He
drew his curved scimitar, and after giving a
glance at the four rope-bound sailors, who
naturally were so scared at the idea of Algerian
slavery that true terror was depicted in their
countenances, and also at their three guards,
in masquerade dresses, who kept their pistols
pointed at the supposed captives with admirable
fierceness, he addressed me some question or
other in his abominable lingo.

" I felt that all was lost, unless I played my
part properly, and, summoning to my mind all
the Turkish words I ever knew, I stood majes-
tically erect, placed my left hand across my
breast, looked at one of his eyes (at both it
was impossible), and pointing emphatically
with my right to myself, I exclaimed, 'Os-
manlee!' then, slowly pointing to the four
sailors, I hissed out with the most demoniacal
sneer I could muster, 'Giaour!' The Moor
burst into a loud laugh, and made another
unintelligible speech. 1 laughed responsively,

and made him a long reply in gibberish, for I dared not use French, lest he might know enough of that language to detect the *ruse*, and at the end I made him a solemn Oriental salaam.

" The poor man was fairly puzzled. It was evident that he thought us Turks; but why did we speak so different a language from his own ? Could we be true believers from some distant province in which some peculiar dialect prevailed ? How came we in this small craft ? How came our dresses to be so magnificently clean ?

" While many such thoughts were no doubt crossing his brain, our félouque had drifted towards the stern of the sloop. I touched my Moorish friend lightly on the arm, and, leading him to the fore part of the félouque, I took up a coil of rope that lay there, and, uncoiling it, fastened one end to a stake projecting on our deck, and the other I threw on board the sloop. I then by signs, accompanied by much jabbering, made him understand, as well as I could, that I wished his vessel to tow us after it, and so for him to take possession both of the félouque and of the four 'Giaours.' The idea seemed to please him. He grinned, and climbing up to his own craft gave orders which resulted in attaching the connecting rope on board the sloop, and so we followed in his wake. Night was approaching, and, as the weather was gloomy, it was not long before we were enveloped in darkness. At the earliest moment that I thought it prudent, we cut the rope and parted company from our piratical consort, very glad *d'en être quitte à si bon marché.* We safely arrived at Bastia, where we narrated our adventure, to the great amusement of our friends, and spent a merry Carnival."

Mr. U. " Truly a wonderful escape ! "

De L. " I have had many much more wonderful escapes. In the year 1720, when the big South Sea Bubble and hundreds of its progeny of infant bubbles burst—"

I. (Anxious to nip this other adventure in the bud.) " Oh, what a year of excitement it must have been ! Were you in the thick of it ? "

De L. " I was. One afternoon, I was returning home from Jonathan's very melancholy, for on that day I had lost my third fortune—"

A. "Your third fortune, Chevalier! How shocking!"

I. "Yes, indeed. Pray tell us how fortunes were made and lost at that eventful period."

Mrs. U. "Pray let the Chevalier finish the story that he was commencing."

De L. "Since Miss Alice deigns to take an interest in my fortunes and their vicissitudes, I may explain to her that I became by turns a rich and a poor man three times within the space of a few months."

Mr. U. "I suppose in connexion with the speculations of that notorious year. I remember reading about them in the Weekly Journal, but as I myself took no part in them I shall not be sorry to learn something of the secret machinery, the hidden cranks and wheels, by which the juggle was performed, from one who has been behind the scenes."

De L. "Alas! sir, it was less the ingenuity of the contrivers than it was the madness of the public that caused the mischief. An insane desire of becoming suddenly rich took possession of high and low. The epidemic had commenced in my charming *patrie*,

France, and thence it spread to this country, where it raged with increased intensity."

Mr. U. " A. French disease, but of Scotch origin through John Law."

De L. " For a couple of years I had invested my small savings in South Sea Stock, at the moderate rates then current, and was quite content with the fair interest I received; but early in 1720 the price had risen so high, under the influence of the increasing mania for jobbing in it, that I determined to sell my stock, and the modest 800*l.* I held realized nearly 4,000*l.*, a sum which to me was wealth. That I call my fortune number one. Happy if I had remained contented with it ! "

I. " And what did you do with the money ? "

De L. " Just so. How to invest the money was my difficulty and my danger. I determined to consult an old friend of mine who was doing an extensive business at Jonathan's Coffee House, as a stockjobber. He was a Jew whom I had known in Paris under the name of De Castro; and I had then rendered him an essential service by assisting his escape from France."

I. "Had he then been guilty of some offence?"

DE L. "Nothing serious. A mere infringement of some legal form in the details of his business, which was being daily committed by others. But they being Christians it was overlooked; and he being a Jew, hated for his religion and envied for his success, it brought him in difficulties with Monsieur l'Intendant de la Police. As he knew that he would be heavily fined, De Castro hastily remitted all his funds to a friend in London, and followed them there himself. Not long afterwards, I also came over to settle here. De Castro found me out, and requited my services to him by many good offices and useful introductions, and we remained excellent friends. He had adopted here the name of Castrow, and was supposed to have acquired considerable wealth. To this friend I addressed myself for advice how to lay out my money to the best advantage.

"'First of all,' said he, 'you must be cool —cool as a cucumber. These are exciting times, and there is a heap of money to be made; but, if you get flustered and fiery, you are lost. Let "cucumber" be your motto.

Whenever I have been tempted to act rashly, or say " yes " too quickly, " cucumber " have I muttered to myself, and have refrained. Cucumber has saved me from no end of losses. Therefore, Chevalier, let us say " cucumber " together, and consider your case.'

" I told him what I had done, and how much I had realized, adding that I wanted him to guide me as to the best mode of investing my 4,000*l.*

" ' There are fifty ways,' said he ; ' but most of them are dangerous. A number of new and wild projects are being daily started, which I would not touch with the tongs. Several are at a premium, but there will be a reaction and they will collapse. None of these for me. " Cucumber " is my motto, and caution my pilot. You sold your South Sea Stock at 402 ; well, do you think that it will go on rising for ever and ever ? Certainly not ; a fall must come, and on that we must base our operations. Your course is clear. Go in as a bear ! '

" On my expressing my utter ignorance as to how or why I was to assume the shape of that animal, he explained,—

" 'You have heard of the hunter who sold the bear's skin first, and then set to work to catch the bear; well, so you must sell S. S. S. (short for South Sea Stock) for delivery in a fortnight. This you can do to-day at 407. By that time it may be down to 300. Then you buy it at that figure, and deliver it at 400, making 100*l.* profit on every 400*l.* you have sold. A valuable bear's skin it will be, will it not?—what I call a nice little operation in furriery.'

" 'But,' I asked, ' supposing that, during the fortnight, the price of S. S. S. should rise instead of falling?'

" 'Oh!' replied he, 'if you are for the rise, that is a different thing, and you should buy instead of selling. But a rise is out of the question. S. S. S. has advanced from 112 to 407 in a run, and reaction is sure to set in. You must be cool. Only excited fools believe in a perpetual advance of prices. As soon believe that a rocket will never come down. Say " cucumber," and believe in reaction.'

"I yielded to his superior knowledge and coolness, and instructed him to sell the bear's-skin, and be sure to catch the bear in good time.

"'Do not fear,' said he; 'I am not one to leave things to the last moment. The instant I see a fair margin of profit for you I will make the purchase against the sale, even though it were ten days before it be required, and even if I had reason to believe that your profit would be larger by waiting. Whenever tempted to increase my risks in order to increase my gains, I steady myself, cry "cucumber," and go in for prudence and moderation.'

"To cut the story short, that perverse S. S. S. continued to advance instead of falling, and at the end of the fortnight the operation was closed, and I lost 3,000*l.* by it. Of course, Castrow was utterly disgusted. He showed me clearly that the Stock ought to have gone down; that it was driven up by a parcel of excited fools, to whom the coolness of cucumber was utterly unknown; and that I should see shortly that he was quite right. Meanwhile, however, my money was gone, and thus I made and lost my first fortune. I fear I shall tire you if I go on to describe my two other rises and falls."

ALL OF US. "No; pray go on. Let us hear all your ups and downs."

DE L. " Some of you must remember, all of you must have heard of, the general infatuation that prevailed .that year. The most ridiculous projects were mooted and adopted. Companies were formed, and the shares at once taken up and resold at a premium. Four millions were subscribed—of course on paper —for establishing a general foundry; as much for improving malt liquor; two millions to buy and sell pitch; two millions for suppressing thieves, and insuring against their depredations; two millions to supply Deal with fresh water; ten millions for a royal fishery in Great Britain; three millions for a grand dispensary; in fact, the aggregate amount of capital which the various shareholders were under engagement to subscribe exceeded 500,000,000*l.* But as for some time the shares passed from one to the other at increasing premiums, all who touched them made a profit: and this encouraged them to repeat the process on fresh adventures. New schemes could not be hatched quick enough to meet the demand, and the impatient public taunted the directors

and other schemers with sterility of invention.
To supply this inordinate demand, subscriptions
were demanded for companies, the names and
purposes of which were only to be revealed at
some subsequent period.

"For instance, I remember—I think nearly
verbatim—an advertisement which appeared in
Mist's Journal. It ran thus,—'This day, the
8th instant, at Sam's Coffee House, at three in
the afternoon, a book will be opened for enter-
ing into a joint co-partnership for carrying on
a thing that will turn to the advantage of the
concerned'; and the applicants were innumer-
able.

"One day, before the mania had by any
means reached its height, I received an invitation from my friend Castrow to call on him
without fail that evening at his private house,
a neat little country box in Goodman's Fields.
He received me with open arms. 'Now,
Chevalier,' said he, 'I am going to replace
the 3,000*l.* I was unfortunate enough to be
instrumental in causing you to lose. I have
always considered it a moral debt, which I
was bound to make good.' I was touched
by his generosity, and warmly expressed my

thanks. 'You have not heard from me for
some little while,' continued he, 'because I was
waiting for the proper time to perform that
act of justice. The time has now come, De
Livordy, and I shall henceforth be relieved
from self-reproach.'

"He then opened his desk, took out a
packet, and, presenting it to me, he said,
'Receive this, my friend, as a proof of the
sincerity of my regard.'

"Not doubting but that the packet contained
notes or bills to a large amount, I began to feel
some scruples of delicacy as to receiving it.
But before I could make up my mind Castrow
said, 'Open the packet, Chevalier, and look at
the contents.' I did so; and found in it a
number of square cards, on each of which was
printed the following notice :—' The bearer is
hereby authorized to subscribe 100*l.* to the Globe
Sail-cloth Company, which in due time will be
formed and publicly announced,' signed with
some name which I could not decipher, and
sealed on the left-hand corner with the sign of
the Globe Tavern in wax. I looked at these
cards rather blankly, and my feelings of gratitude received a decided check.

" 'These,' said Castrow, 'are 100 Globe permits, now worth in the open market 15*l.* each.'

" 'Come,' thought I, 'here is at all events
1,500*l.* for me.'

" 'I obtained them for you,' continued
Castrow, 'as a particular favour, from my
friend Blantwell, one of the directors, at the
price of 10*l.* each, so favour me with your note
of hand for 1,000*l.* Even if you sold them this
day there would be a clear gain to you of 500*l.*,
but I strongly advise you not to do so.'

" 'Well,' thought I, 'even 500*l.* is better than
nothing.' I then thanked him, though with
rather less effusion than before, and requested
he would sell them at once for me, and then
hand me the expected 500*l.*

" 'Nonsense, Chevalier!' cried Castrow;
'you have no nerve. I want you to keep
them till they rise to fifty, which they are sure
to do; and then you will just recover the
money which you lost before.'

" 'Is it the cautious Castrow,' said I, 'who
is now for grasping at inordinate profits, even
with increased risks? Where is your coolness? Remember "cucumber!"'"

" 'My friend,' replied Castrow, 'cucumber

is out of season. We must adapt our diet to circumstances. There is at the present time such an influx of fools determined to drop their money that it would be positively wasteful and immoral not to pick it up. Wait a few days, and you will see how Globe permits will rise. They have only just been planted; wait till they grow a little.'

" I followed his advice, and at the end of the ensuing week we sold them at fifty-six, and my 1,000*l*. dilated suddenly into 5,600*l*. A few days after I saw them quoted at sixty-three, and such had become my greed for gain that I almost repented at having sold so soon; and that, messieurs and mesdames, was my second fortune.

" As to my third, I shall not detain you long. Our old friend South Sea Stock had advanced to 640, at which price I, who had beared them at 400, invested in them all my money, by the advice of my friend Castrow, who, having abjured cucumber, seemed now to be fevered by a course of pepper and mustard. He wanted me to swear on the Old Testament not to part with my stock till it reached 1,000. I did not swear, but I acted as if I had. In September our dear S. S. S. kept rising and rising, and those who made money by it spent it freely, revelled in South Sea jewels, set up South Sea coaches, and bought South Sea estates. At the theatres, new pieces, such as 'The Humours of Change Alley' and 'The Stockjobber turned Gentleman,' levelled their satire at the projectors and their dupes. From the pulpits parsons (themselves not quite innocent of speculations) fulminated against Mammon. The print-shops teemed with caricatures about bubble-blowing and pocket-picking. Ballads, in the most abusive and ungrammatical doggrel, were sung about the streets. Packs of bubble-cards were published at 2s. 6d. each, every card having an engraving of some one of the hundred and odd companies that had been started, with a pointless epigram of four lines on it. In society it was not unusual for a lady when playing cards to exclaim, as she played out a knave, 'There's a director for you!'

" But all this raillery had little effect on the busy votaries of speculation. One morning, towards the end of September, I was offered 981½ for my S. S. S. I took time to calculate and consider. A sale at 981½ would have yielded me my third additional fortune—a good 3,000*l.* to append to my previous gains of 5,600*l.*, and I felt very much inclined to accept the offer. But then 981½ was such an odd, queer, uncouth kind of a price. Why not go in for the beautifully simple, clear, round (*totus teres atque rotundus*) figure of 1,000? It was only waiting a few hours. Why should I be so morbidly anxious to clutch at my gold? I was a sober-minded man, and if the price went up to 1,100, as no doubt it would, after I had sold, I should view it with equanimity; but as to selling under 1,000, 'No,' said I to myself; 'round figures for ever! If the man can pay 980 odd, surely he can give the 1,000, unless he is a greedy beast. How men can be such curmudgeons as to lay any stress on such a slight difference is inconceivable to me.'

"So I went back to my buyer, who was waiting patiently for my answer, and I said to him, 'No; I hold for just the round figure of 1,000. That is what I will accept, and no less.' This occurred at Jonathan's during the temporary absence of Castrow. A few minutes afterwards he came in, and I told him of the offer I had refused.

"'Do you know,' said he, 'that I feel a taste of cucumber in my mouth, and if I had been here I should have advised you to sell. I cannot help thinking that we are on the crest of the wave. Go to your buyer, and say you accept his offer.' I did so, but the man had just supplied himself in some other quarter. Next day I was only offered 940, which was of course absurd, having refused 981½ the day before. Day after day prices fell; no one could say why. When the quotation came down to 640, at which I had bought, I became frightened, and determined to sell. But alas! the quotation was a nominal one, and there were no actual buyers. On the 1st of October the stock had fallen to 370, and on the 6th to 180. A panic seized me; I became a frantic seller at any price, and finally accepted 64, which was one-tenth of what I had bought at, and one-fifteenth of what I had been such a fool as to refuse. Thus did I lose my second and third fortune at 'one fell swoop.' And here I am nevertheless, ladies, at your service."

We thanked M. de Livordy very much
for his interesting reminiscences, and, as the
hour was getting late, he made his bow and
departed, leaving us wondering how much of
his narrative was true and how much was
invented.

CHAPTER IV.

I OBTAIN AN APPOINTMENT. 1737.

WHAT my career was to be, my kind guardians had not yet decided. Whether I was to prepare for becoming in due time a general or an admiral, a bishop or a lord chancellor, was still an open question. But, while they were considering the point, an opening presented itself for a clerkship in the War Office, and it was settled that I should condescend to this *ad interim*, if only to keep me from idleness. It was a post in the Flint and Pipeclay Department, requiring no previous knowledge, very little present labour, and affording a gentlemanly position and a gentlemanly income of 300*l.* per annum. How this piece of preferment fell to us, I will tell you.

Sir Robert Walpole had for some time been

under obligations to a parson, the Rev. Arthur Sturrell, for having procured him two votes at a critical stage of the Excise Bill, and had promised on his word of honour (a simple promise would have been breakable) that Sturrell should have the earliest preferment in Walpole's gift that did not exceed 300*l.* a year.

At one of the many jovial dinners given by the convivial Minister, the parson, who was a merry toper, was one of the guests. In the midst of the feast, when each man had got well into his second bottle, Walpole receives a dispatch. With a brief apology he opens it, and, tossing the paper on to the floor, exclaims in his jolly way, " It 's only a trumpery 300*l.* a year. Who will have it ? " A general chorus of " I ! " But, when the noise subsided a little, our parson cried out, " Sir Robert, I claim it ! Hold to your word. I was to have the first 300*l.* a year that came in your way." " By ——, parson, you are right ! I owe it you, and you shall have it. But, mind, you take it for better, for worse, as you do a wife." " You say it is 300*l.* a year ? " " Yes, it is." " All right. I can't get better, and I don't want worse ; so book it to me." " Very well ! Mind it is in extinction of all claims. Gentlemen, you all bear witness to this?" "Yes, yes." "Very well, it's a bargain. Sturrell, let us shake hands upon it." The parson shook hands and asked, "Where is the living situated, Sir Robert?" "Living! who said it was a living? Why, it's a clerkship in the Flint and Pipeclay Office!" A loud roar of laughter at the parson's expense followed this announcement. "Oh, but I did not mean that," said Sturrell; "I thought that it was a Church living!" "That's your look-out; I never said so." "But I cannot be a clerk in an office?" "Why not? What prevents you from being parson and clerk too?" "If," said another, "instead of the Pipeclay, it had been the Clay-pipe Office, it would have suited the parson better." And the poor parson had to endure more jeering and laughter. All his efforts to cancel his bargain proved fruitless. Sir Robert, whose delight at having outwitted the parson was boundless, proved inexorable. "I'll tell you what, in two words," said he; "it's that or nothing. You wanted 300*l.* a year, and you have got it. If you cannot use the nomination yourself, sell it. We don't care who goes in, provided he is anything decent." With

that Sturrell had to be content. He did sell it
for 400*l.* to an old lady, who made a birthday
present of it to her son, who handed it in pay-
ment of a debt of honour to a Captain Sel-
lowes, who owed my uncle 300*l.*, with two
years' accumulated interest. In cancelment of
this debt, which he considered a very doubtful
one, my uncle gladly accepted the nomination
in question, and, after a few formalities, I was
without much difficulty installed into my new
post.

If any sour-minded economist should take
exception to an office where so much was spent
and so little was done, let him feel rebuked
when he learns that matters were much worse
a few years before. Then there were two
separate departments—one for flints to arm
the muskets, and one for pipeclay to adorn the
musketeers. Then there were two sets of
offices, two sets of clerks, and, of course,
double the amount of expenditure.

By an effort of patriotism and an abnega-
tion of patronage that was quite unprecedented,
the Minister consolidated the two establish-
ments, and saved the country 2,500*l.* per
annum.

But the clever Minister made good political capital out of his virtuous act. Whenever accused of extravagance, he only had to quote his consolidation of the Flint and Pipeclay Departments as an instance of his zeal for " reducing expenditure without impairing efficiency," and the accuser was silenced. The case was made a stalking-horse to ride down and trample on the Opposition whenever they inveighed against waste and peculation. This saving of 2,500*l.* cost the country at least ten times the amount. It atoned for a multitude of jobs, just as cheap charity covers a multitude of lucrative sins.

The Chevalier de Livordy continued to spend an occasional evening with us, and to entertain us with his inexhaustible budget of stories. Part of their merit, no doubt, consisted in his charming way of telling them; a voice, gentle, but varied; little gesture, but that very expressive; and just enough inflection of tone and glance of the eye to mark his points,—never enough to exaggerate them.

I must give you one more sample of these pleasant evenings.

Mrs. U. " I have been this morning to make some purchases, for the first time, at the new Fleet Market, opened the other day by Sir John Bernard, the Lord Mayor, instead of the old Stocks' Market, defunct."

Mr. U. " You may add, and in the place of the old Fleet Ditch, buried ; and a good thing, too ! Let us say, *Requiescat in pace,* without adding, *Resurgat ;* for a viler infliction on the nostrils than that huge gutter of filth never disgraced the name of river. Why the *Cloaca maxima* must have been lavender-water compared with it."

De L. " I cannot say that I view the disappearance of the old old Flete with unmixed feelings ; and I am glad that they have only arched it over as far as Fleet Street. One may, at least, still trace its course into the Thames. I rather grudge the gradual encroachments of new on old London. Why, they will be pulling down London Bridge next. We are getting into the new, the bare, and the stiff, instead of the ancient, the picturesque, and the genial. What will our modern poets do without the river Flete ? See how Dryden, Pope, Gay, Garth, and others revelled in its turbid stream !

I hope, madam, that the new market answered your expectations."

Mrs. U. " It did not. There was a little fruit on sale, but scarcely any meat or fish. I fancy dealers do not easily take to new markets. Then the booths are poor constructions, not above ten or twelve feet in height."

De L. " There was a stipulation made that the booths should not exceed fifteen feet. The market charter provides for that."

Mrs. U. " Besides which, the incessant hammering at the numerous undertakers' shops, scattered up and down the street, was quite distressing."

De L. " Bad enough ; but not quite so bad as the din of the coppersmiths in Houndsditch. Strange how particular trades affect particular streets."

Mr. U. " So Bucklersbury is full of herb-shops ; but that is accounted for by its vicinity to the Stocks' Market. Hence Shakspeare's allusion to the smell of ' Bucklersbury in simpling time.' So an old dramatist, I think Webster, says, ' Go into Bucklersbury, and fetch me two ounces of preserved melons.' "

I. " But, of all thoroughfares, I should have

thought London Bridge the noisiest, from the incessant uproar of the traffic day and night."

DE L. "Mr. Frank is right. The noise is like the continuous rush of a cataract. But I understand that the inhabitants get so accustomed to it, that they cannot sleep in the country because it is so quiet."

MR. U. "London Bridge is, beyond controversy, the most frequented thoroughfare in the world; and the stream of traffic is as inexhaustible as the waters of a river. '*Labitur et labetur in omne volubilis ævum.*' Rome had several bridges; London has but one. It is the only *vinculum* or connecting link between one side of the river and the other for half a million of human beings—a narrow isthmus between two continents."

DE L. "Besides, the road is so narrow, on account of the houses, that it never exceeds twenty feet, and in some places contracts to twelve; so that although no space is reserved for foot-passengers, and the entire width is allotted to horse traffic, this can only creep along like a funeral procession spun out interminably."

MRS. U. "There is some talk, I have heard,

of widening the road by pulling down the houses on the bridge."

A. " Oh, what a desecration! I hope that they will never do that. Those dear, old, quaint, rumshackled, picturesque houses, with their lofty arches thrown over from one side of the street to the other like rainbows! And then the old chapel on the centre pier, and Nonsuch House! Surely they can never be such Goths as to destroy all those beautiful objects."

MR. U. " Just like these foolish, impulsive, adorable women! They infinitely prefer a lot of mouldy, dilapidated, unwholesome, and tottering tenements to convenience, usefulness, health, and safety. Are you aware, daughter of mine, that the only secure plan for a foot-passenger to cross the bridge is to follow behind a carriage or cart, and take his chance of the horse that comes behind biting a piece out of his shoulder?"

A. " Why not take refuge in a shop when the crush becomes dangerous?"

MR. U. " And stay there till all the carriages have gone by? Wait, like ' *rusticus, dum defluit amnis* '? Thank you, dear! I should have to bid an eternal adieu to Red Lion Square."

DE L. "It is in serious contemplation to have a second bridge over the Thames, somewhere about Westminster. It is being designed by Mr. Labelye, and will probably be commenced in another year or two."

MR. U. "So I hear; and it will be an immense relief to the traffic over London Bridge, which, already enormous, is increasing, and will soon become unmanageable."

DE L. "And yet, in spite of this enormous traffic, it is not many years since I performed a curious feat. In April, 1722, in company with some other gentlemen, I dined in the middle of the London Bridge roadway. You may smile, my good friends, but it was so. It was at two o'clock in the afternoon, in the open air, in the middle of the street, and near the centre arch of the bridge. We had a large table set up, were waited on by three or four servants, and we remained for four hours over our wine and punch."

OMNES. "Oh, Chevalier! Oh, M. de Livordy! Come, that is too much!"

DE L. "It is the literal truth. The feast was given by Baldwin, the rich hosier, in front of his own house on London Bridge; and there was no small crowd round us to enjoy the sight."

Mrs. U. " But were you not run into by the carts and other vehicles ?"

De L. " They left us quite unmolested."

I. " Were you acting under the authority of either Government or the civic body ?"

De L. " No ; it was quite a private dinner."

A. " Was there a chain or a barrier thrown across the entrance of the bridge to stop the traffic on that day ?"

De L. " There was neither chain nor barrier to obstruct the entrance. The traffic stopped of its own accord."

Omnes. " Then we give it up."

De L. " The solution is simple. The central drawbridge had got out of order, and during the few days required for its repair the bridge ceased to be a thoroughfare ; and although there was no physical obstruction to carriages, &c., yet they, of course, kept away, having notice that the bridge could not be crossed."

Mr. U. " You did right to tell us quickly, or we should very soon have guessed it."

De L. " I am not sure of that. You were half disposed to look upon it as a little romance of my invention. It is not those enigmas which have the most simple solution that are most easily deciphered, as witness the egg of Columbus. In fact, I was nearly led into a duel through a perplexing circumstance, that proved simple enough when explained. Shall I tell you what it was ? "

Mrs. U. " Do, pray, Chevalier."

De L. " When I lived at Paris I frequented the Café Colbert. One evening a well-dressed young man, with one eye, came in and seated himself at my table. He would have been a fine-looking fellow, but for an ugly black patch over his right eye. Two days afterwards we met again at the same place, and got on speaking terms; and in about a week we became very friendly. He was well informed on general topics, but very reserved as to his own affairs ; and all I gathered from him was that his name was Gudaine, and that he was staying in Paris for a little time on private business. The next day I was dining with four other friends at the Couteau d'Or, when one of them, Capitaine Rodevin, casually re-marked that he had three or four times dined in this same place with a one-eyed young man who, though a provincial, seemed a well-bred and gentlemanly fellow. I pricked up my ears, and asked,—

" 'Do you know his name? Was it Gudaine?'

" 'Yes,' said the Capitaine; 'that's the man.'

" 'Curious! I too have met him several times at the Café Colbert, and have made his acquaintance.'

" 'Ah! and do you not agree with me, Chevalier, that he is a very pleasant companion?'

" 'I do, indeed, Capitaine, and were it not for that ugly black patch over his right eye he would be a noble-looking—'

" 'Stop!' cried the Capitaine; 'you mean his left eye.'

" 'Not at all: I said his right eye, and I mean it.'

" 'Excuse me; you could not have observed him properly, or you have forgotten. I assure you that it is the left eye.'

" 'I am sorry to say, my dear Capitaine, that you are quite wrong. I took particular notice; for his habit was to lean on his right elbow, and rest his diseased eye with the patch on the palm of his right hand, while he used his left to convey his cup of coffee to his mouth.'

" 'You have dreamed it, my good friend, and I will prove it. You see, gentlemen, that little table in the corner, near the window. Now, observe, Gudaine always seats himself at that table, with his back to the wall, and in that position his diseased eye is always next to the window. Now you can see yourselves that in such case it must be the left eye.'

" 'Well,' said they, ' it looks like it, certainly.'

" 'How could it possibly be the right eye?'

" I was nettled at this persistency in wrong, for that he was wrong I felt as certain as of my own existence, and I said with some warmth,—

" 'I affirm, in the most positive manner, that it is Mr. Gudaine's right eye that is affected; and no doubt Monsieur le Capitaine has mistaken that corner of the room for the opposite corner, where it would be the right eye that was nearest the window.'

" 'I am docile under contradiction when I

am in the wrong; but when I am right—and I
generally am—I am not the man to submit to
it. Do you mean to say, sir, that I do not
know the difference between my right and my
left hand?'

"'I always thought you did, up to this
moment; now I have my doubts.'

"'*Morbleu, c'est trop fort!* I cannot brook
this insult, and—'

"'Stop, stop, friends!' interposed the eldest
among us, the Vicomte de Baspré, who saw
that we were on the verge of a serious quarrel:
'one would think that the object of your
dispute were Helen of Troy, or some living
lady of equal charms, whereas really it is only
the ugly black patch over the eye of a man.
A very unworthy *casus belli!* In such a cause,
stake gold, not life. Rodevin,' he continued,
addressing the Capitaine, 'will you bet De
Livordy a louis d'or that you are
right?'

"'Willingly,' replied he.

"'Done!' said I.

"'Jules,' cried the Capitaine to the waiter,
'you know that one-eyed gentleman that I
sometimes dine with at the corner table?'

" ' Yes, sir,' replied the waiter; ' Mr. Gudaine, is it not ? '

" ' The same. Well, let me know when he makes his appearance.'

" ' He has just come in, sir, through the other door.'

" ' Ah ! then present to him my compliments, as well as those of the Chevalier de Livordy, and beg that he will do us the honour of joining us here.'

" Accordingly, in a few moments, the waiter returned, followed by Mr. Gudaine, to whom he was showing the way to our table. But what was our astonishment when we found that now Mr. Gudaine had no black patch on either eye ! Could it be the right man ? Yes, it was ; for he came up and bowed to us both in the most friendly manner, saying, with a cordial laugh,—

" ' I see, gentlemen, that you are looking hard at my eyes, and are wondering at the marvellously sudden cure that has restored my sight. But I will explain all. For family reasons, which it is superfluous to relate, I had to disguise myself for a few days until a reconciliation took place between two relations. That disguise I effected by means of the black patch that you saw on one of my eyes. The two relations are now reconciled; I am the happiest of men, and I am heartily glad at being able to throw off that disgusting and troublesome deformity.'

"We congratulated Mr. Gudaine at his relief from what might truly be called a terrible eyesore, and hoped for the continuance of his friendship.

"'But,' added I, 'I have a bet of a louis d'or with my friend, le Capitaine Rodevin here, as to which was the eye on which you wore the patch—the right or the left. Perhaps you will be good enough to tell us, and decide who is the winner of the bet. Do you agree, Capitaine?'

"'Yes,' replied the Capitaine; 'I am quite content to abide by Mr. Gudaine's decision.'

"'You have both won, gentlemen.'

"'How can that be?'

"'I found it exceedingly uncomfortable, as well as very injurious to the sight, to have always the same eye bunged up; so, from time to time, I removed the black patch from one eye to the other; but, to lessen the chances of detection, I always contrived to present the same appearance at the same place. Hence it was that I invariably placed the patch on my right eye when I visited the Café Colbert, and on my left eye when I visited the Couteau d'Or. I therefore, gentlemen, consider your bet as a drawn one.'

" We were much amused at this unexpected issue to our dispute, and ended by spending a pleasant and jovial evening with our new friend."

Mr. U. " Very good indeed. Moral: never make too sure of anything."

De Livordy did not remain much longer; but I remember that, among other curious matters with which he entertained us, he stated that, some fifteen or twenty years before, several of the newspapers, by way of sign or motto, had the following woodcut on the top of their first page :—

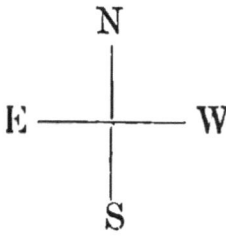

thereby giving their readers to understand that they communicated NEWS from the four quarters of the globe. Very ingenious and very pithy; but unfortunately it displayed the same defect as, no doubt, their intelligence often did—viz., inaccuracy; for it will be observed that the east was placed where the west should be, and, if the cardinal points were set with astronomical precision, the reading would be altered to NWES.

CHAPTER V.

CHARLEY FRAMPTON had left Dr. Burridge's
school a year before I did; but, on my taking
up my residence at my uncle's, we renewed
our acquaintance and often met. I introduced
him to our circle; but my aunt did not much
fancy him, partly on account of his dashing,
flippant, and scoffing manner, but chiefly because he was the son of that Whig and Hanoverian *par excellence*, Mr. Frampton of the
Secret Service Office. She consequently did
not, although always civil to him, much encourage his visits.

I, however, occasionally spent a few hours
with him, to enjoy his lively sallies; for, however satirical he might be in his remarks about
others, to me he was always friendly and good

natured. One evening that I called on him at his chambers—for he did not live with his father, being supposed to be too hard at work studying for the law to lose his time in the domestic circle—I found him in high glee.

" Frank," he exclaimed, " I am so glad you have come. You know my fondness for eccentric characters. I stumbled on one two days ago that is quite adorable."

" What, some great author? Perhaps a poet ? "

" Bah ! take the pen from between their fingers, and authors, as a rule, are the most commonplace of beings. No ; my hero is a shop-boy."

" What ? "

" Just so — a shop-boy. Imagine a big shock of tangled, bright red hair overhanging a bony, angular face buttered over with freckles, and supported by a tall, lean, loose-jointed body ; the whole being the property of an ill-dressed lad of about sixteen."

" Well, Charley, I see nothing so enchanting in all that."

" No more did I at first. I was strolling about Aldersgate Street—you know what a

lonely, out-of-the-way place it is, as deserted as
if all the residents had died of the plague, and
all the houses were to let—when this raw youth
comes up to me, and, knocking his forehead
with his forefinger by way of salute, says,
' Please, sir, which is Sadler's Wells ? ' The
plumpness of the question amused me, for it
implied that one of the surrounding buildings
must be the theatre in question, and that I only
had to point at it with my finger to satisfy the
querist. I determined to undeceive him as to
the immediate propinquity of Sadler's Wells,
and therefore answered him, ' Sadler's Wells,
my man, is at Pimlico.' ' Where 's that ? ' he
innocently asked. ' Near Wapping,' was my
reply. ' Then Wapping 's moved,' said he ;
' cos it used to be on the old river, while
Sadler's Wells is on the New River.' I answered with a fresh mystification ; but I found
my friend, with all his grammatical heresies,
quite able to bandy jokes with me, and, in
short, he took my fun so good-humouredly,
and displayed so much barbaric originality and
quaintness, that I not only conducted him to
Sadler's Wells, but paid for two pit tickets and
went in with him. During the time that

elapsed before the performances commenced—
for we were full early—I elicited from him
that he was shop-boy to Mr. and Mrs. Reffs
the grocer in Long Lane, and that this half-
holiday was given him because he had 'put
them up to a thing or two.' I then extracted
from him full details about this 'thing or two,'
and when I came home I committed it all
to paper. Would you like to read it? I hope
that you will say yes, as that is what I wrote
it for. Besides, it is highly moral, which, St.
Francis! is quite in your line. It shows what
the lottery mania is leading us to."

"A very laudable object. We who live on
the mere surface of the community take too
little heed as to what is passing in the depths
below."

" Of course I prefer spending my life among
the luxurious hundreds; but I do like an occasional deep dive among the millions, and
observe their particular ways of preying on
each other. Deceit and humbug are just as
rife with them as with us; but then they assume novel and grotesque shapes which it is
very interesting to contemplate."

"But surely, friend, this is not an exact report of what your red-haired phenomenon imparted to you ? "

" Not quite; but the pith and substance is his, and I have only put it into shape, and thrown in a dash of colour here and there."

I read the paper, and, finding it rather droll, I transcribe it here as a sample of Charley's style, and a sketch of the humours of the times :—

DRAMATIS PERSONÆ.

MR. REFFS, *a grocer, with an increasing family and a decreasing trade.*

MRS. REFFS, *his wife, who has touching reminiscences of past grandeur when lady's maid to Lady Griggs.*

SHIRTY, *their shop-boy—a workhouse foundling.*
  Mr. C. Frampton's red-haired phenomenon.

SCENE.—*The back parlour of a grocer's shop in Long Lane, Smithfield.*

Enter MR. *and* MRS. REFFS.

MR. REFFS. My dear, I am sorry to inform you that our takings to-day are worse than ever,—two and twopence in cash, four and fourpence on credit!

Mrs. Reffs. What's come to the place? You used, at one time, to take your regular twenty and thirty shillings a day in bright silver.

Reffs. And yet I work harder, sell cheaper, and talk civiller than I ever did. I never made such a lovely show in the window. That barley-sugar church steeple draws a crowd of people to look at it outside; but, hang it, they don't come in.

Mrs. R. I'll tell you what it is; we are not low enough for the neighbourhood. We're too genteel for Long Lane. If I could force my nature to be low, we'd get on like blazes.

Reffs. I don't think it's that. I'm afraid it's those Hickses. Bother them! why didn't they set up their new shop in the next parish?

Mrs. R. It's quite impossible that can be the cause. Why, I know positively that Mrs. Hicks was a kitchen-maid.

Reffs. That's no odds. Our customers are civil enough, find no fault, and give no reasons; but I know, through Shirty, that many of them have left us to go to the Hickses.

Mrs. R. How does Shirty know?

Reffs. Shirty is an idle rascal, but as sharp as vinegar and as quick as a minnow. The rogue eats our figs, and sucks our sugar, but he sticks up for the old shop like a Nero. He has watched on the sly, and has seen lots of our customers—aye, some of them that owe us money too—sneak into the new shop ten doors off.

Mrs. R. Shameful!—to leave an old respectable concern like ours, for that dirty, new-fangled booth,—for it's little else; and Mrs. Hicks dressing as slovenly as she does, and her hair's not knowing the touch of a comb for weeks!

Reffs. There must be some reason; and Shirty has a notion about it which may not be so very far from the mark.

Mrs. R. And what is that?

Reffs. Very absurd, you'll say; but there may be something in it. Hicks has got painted up over his door, "Hicks, lottery grocer," and sticks in his window a notice that buyers at his shop will have the chance of getting a prize of twenty guineas at a lottery to be drawn at his shop at Christmas.

Mrs. R. What nonsense! You know that the lottery will never be drawn; or, if it is, the prize will never be paid.

Reffs. I know? Well, mayhap I do. But what's the use of my knowing it, if other people don't? If they are took in, meanwhile we suffer.

Mrs. R. But what a low, mean, base, shabby mode of doing business!

Reffs. Scandalous! Of course, no respectable tradesman could descend to such vile tricks.

Mrs. R. It's little better than swindling! I have read about these little-go lotteries in the papers, decoying poor people to their ruin, and tempting servants to rob their employers to buy tickets.

Reffs. Devil's engines for turning honest men into rogues!

Mrs. R. Cheating never prospers! Hicks will suffer for this.

Reffs. No doubt: they'll catch it hot some day. But, mean time, the wretches are kidnapping our customers.

Mrs. R. Let them. The day of reckoning will come upon them like a thief in the night!

REFFS. Very like; but, meanwhile, where are we to get the money to pay our rent?

MRS. R. Rent! what's rent compared with virtue? Let's do what is right, John, and trust the Lord for our rent.

REFFS. All very fine, but the landlord won't trust us for it. Not but what I'd cut off my hand sooner than demean myself to such low shifts; but what are we to do?

MRS. R. Write a letter to Hicks, and explain calmly to him what a vile, dishonourable thing it is of him to entice our customers away by such disgraceful tricks. Ask him in a friendly manner whether he is aware that he has a soul to be saved, and whether he is going about it the right way. Show him what he ought—

REFFS. Pshaw! my dear, that will never do. He would only laugh at us. Suppose we call Shirty in, and cross-examine him about this matter?

MRS. R. Very well, as you like. But, John, keep a sharp look-out after this lad; he may, for aught you know, be robbing the till to put into lotteries himself.

REFFS. All right. Shirty!

Enter SHIRTY, *with a shutter on his shoulder.*

SHIRTY. Door is open, please, and three more shutters to put up. Shall I leave them and come to you, or leave you and go to them ?

REFFS. Finish closing, of course.

S. As you please ; people might still come in. Hicks's is wide open, with a flaring brass lamp.

MRS. R. We are not bound to go by what is done at such low places. Respectable shops close at this hour.

S. All right. Only I knows of a pound of dips and three red herrings as went past us on Tuesday night, cos we was shut. [*Exit* SHIRTY.

MRS. R. That's the worst of having to cope with these common people. They are at it early and late. They run your legs off to keep up with them. No wonder they can't find time to wash their faces.

REFFS. Dodd, the barber, tells me that Hicks never goes to him, but, like a miserly screw, shaves himself. What a mean trick !

Re-enter SHIRTY.

S. I've shut up; so you're quite safe from any more bizness to-night. Shall I go down and get my supper ?

REFFS. Stay a moment, Shirty. You had an idea, you told me, that the Hickses got our customers away by means of their lottery scheme. But surely people are not such fools as to be taken in by that?

S. Ain't they, though? Lord love you, they 're much bigger fools than they need be for that. It 's a sure bait to trap them. I 've heerd of things a thousand times less treackly than that catching heaps of flies.

MRS. R. But you know that the lottery will never be drawn, nor the prize paid. They 're sure to find some way of sneaking out of it.

S. Mayhap they may, but then there 's the chance. Now, you see, I have been told when speaking to myself that I 'm no fool; and yet if I had groceries to buy I 'd go to Hicks's, and not here.

MRS. R. What! you would leave the old shop!

S. Why not? If I was an outsider, with money in my pocket, I 'd spend it where I got most for it. Why should I stick to the old shop for better or worse? If I 've been an old customer, and spent lots at the old shop, why then it 's the old shop that owes me the turn.

I'm not bound to throw up twenty guineas for the sake of the old shop.

REFFS. You talk of twenty guineas, Shirty, as if you were sure of them, whereas you know it's ten thousand to one if you ever get them.

S. What o' that? Who stays counting up by clock-work what the chances is or isn't? The ghost of a chance is enough. People doats on a chance, and don't stop to put it in the scales to see how much it weighs. If for ninepence a man can buy a pound of sugar at your shop, and a pound of sugar, with a chance to boot, at Hicks's, why, in course, he goes to the lottery-shop.

REFFS. Confound those lottery-shops and lotteries altogether!

S. All right; but they go in and win all the same. There's no fun in coming to our shop. People swap their money for our pepper, and it's all over. But at Hicks's, for the same money, they get as much pepper, and the fun of having something to dream about besides.

REFFS. To dream about, yes; and it's nothing but a dream!

S. What does it matter? That's quite enough for a chap to hug and fondle and coddle up in his mind, so that, for the time, it's as good as real to him. It's like a doll girls toss about and fancy a live baby. And then it lasts such a while! One night we lies awake, and sets our wits to work as to what we shall do with the twenty guineas when we gets 'em. Oh! so and so. Next night we spend it quite a different way; and before the time comes, we've spent it in make-believe a hundred times over. Law love you, if the twenty guineas never does come at all, we've had all its worth in fun and fancy; and all this you get at Hicks's for nothing.

Mrs. R. It's a deceitful snare, and people ought to know better.

S. Ought! "Ought" is a nasty word. It always means that you're to do something you don't like, such as "You ought to take a dose of jalap." "You ought to listen to the sarmon and not go asleep." "You ought to love a chap that's boxed your ears." "You ought to pay your debts, though you've no money." Well, one good thing is that "oughting" don't do much; people go their own way in spite of it.

Reffs. Now look here, Shirty; what do you

think is the best thing to be done to meet this
crooked way of luring customers?

S. Why, to take to it yourself, to be sure.
You're now fighting with your fists agin a man
as fights with a sword. You take to the sword
too, and you'll win the day.

REFFS. If one could only be persuaded that
it was genteel, one might just look at the idea
and turn it over.

S. Genteel! why, what can be more tip-top,
red-hot genteel than the king? And see what
a lot of money he's making by his lotteries!
Why they tell me he couldn't pay his butcher's
bills without them. And who are you for to
say that it's wrong to do what King George
does? Why, it's flat mutiny!

MRS. R. I suppose that there are some respectable shops that have taken to this sort of
thing?

S. Hundreds, and soon will be thousands.
Why, some of the very high-class trades have
gone into it. I knows lots of lottery-tailors
and lottery-drapers; and I've heerd, but
ain't sure, that there's a lottery-banker: but,
if you go downwards, you'll find them in
every alley. Them's the chaps that are

sucking away all the trade from you stiff uns.

Mrs. R. It is hard lines to see your business walking away from you.

S. Walking!—running, you mean. There's a barber in Ram Court that's just a-coining of money. His charge is twopence for a shave, but he gives a prize of ten pounds. He has ten times the custom he had when he only charged a penny.

Reffs. If it was not like going down in the eyes of the world, why—

S. Going down? Not a bit! It's up you go in the eyes of the world, if you sacks the money. It ain't like swimming, but just the other way. Empty pockets sink you. Lots of gold buoys you up, and keeps you up. Tell you what, master, you just go in for the lottery dodge, and my wages will be riz in a month.

Reffs. It might be worth considering.

Mrs. R. If it could be done in some new way; some higher style, as it were—more dignified, more—

S. Tell you what. Put up a hundred bags —pound bags—of moist sugar, and stick up a notice as there's a guinea-piece in one of them—you don't know which—and the lucky finder may keep it.

REFFS. Nonsense ! what should I get by that ? I should not make a guinea's profit out of the whole boiling.

S. (*contemptuously*). Why, of course I never meant that the guinea should be there ! It's only giving old Mrs. Rimmer, the charwoman, a shilling to say that she got the lucky bag and sacked the guinea. Then you could play the same game over again, and your sugar would all go off in a twinkling.

REFFS. You wicked boy, that would be cheating ! I would sooner starve.

MRS. R. Well, I don't know; people would get their full money's worth in sugar, and I 'm sure it would be a charity to poor Mrs. Rimmer to enable her to earn an honest shilling.

S. To be sure it would. But if you 're squeamish, and want to do the thing grand, let 's look out for some other dodge.

MRS. R. Suppose we published to the world that to the largest buyer in the course of a year at our shop we should, every Christmas, present gratis a—well—a shagreen snuff-box ?

S. Who do you think would put themselves out of the way for a fourpenny box? Besides, all the small buyers would keep away, 'cos they'd no chance. Now they all gets a chance at Hicks's,—large and small.

REFFS. Can't you, Shirty, find something feasible to propose? How slow you are! You might have thought of a dozen things by this.

S. (*slapping his forehead*). I have it; yes, I have it!

MRS. R. Then out with it.

S. This is a dodge, and no mistake. Quite snuffs out old Hicks's rushlight. Quite a big go!

MRS. R. But come, young man, explain what your notion is.

S. Sounds quite grand. Smells of Garraway's and rich Jews.

REFFS. If you don't quickly say what your plan is, why—I'll invent it myself! Now, what is it?

S. Hicks's prize is twenty guineas. You make yours five hundred pounds.

REFFS. Five hundred pounds! You're mad, Shirty. Where the deuce is the money to come from?

S. Out of the six hundred you get, if you have to pay anything at all.

REFFS. I don't understand; do you, my dear?

MRS. R. No, John. I fear the poor lad is crazy.

S. If you pay five hundred pounds you get a hundred by it. So that, unless you lose, you gain nothing.

MR. and MRS. REFFS. (*shaking their heads*). Poor fellow! he's very far gone!

S. You don't see it yet; but you soon will. Now, look here! The first thing you do is to go and buy a sixteenth share of a ticket in the State lottery, say No. 1001. That won't cost much. Then you come back here to blow the trumpet, and make it known far and wide that, in case No. 1001 in the State lottery gets the ten thousand pounds prize, then you bind yourself to put down five hundred pounds as a prize to be drawn for at Christmas by the holders of tickets that you're going to give to every buyer of a guinea's worth of goods at your shop. Now do you see?

REFFS. Oh, yes. Let's see. If No. 1001

comes a blank, then I give tickets, and out of the five hundred I pay six; but, if it turns up a prize, why of course I lose nothing. Something of that sort, wasn't it? You should explain it more clearly. You muddle it up.

S. Why, it's as clear as starch. If No. 1001 wins the big prize, you get six hundred pounds, and give away five hundred out of it; and if it turns up a blank, you give away what you get,—that is, nothing.

Mrs. R. Don't you see? If we give away nothing, we get nothing ourselves: our only hope of getting something is by giving five hundred pounds to our customers.

Reffs. Of course, of course; it's quite simple. As far as I can sum it up, all that we have to lay out is a trifle to pay for a sixteenth share in No. 1001. But, Shirty, why must it be that number, 1001?

S. Any number will do. No. 5,000,000¼ if you like.

Mrs. R. This appears to me a respectable plan. Five hundred pounds is a respectable sum; twenty guineas is low, but five hundred pounds puts it on a respectable footing.

REFFS. I really think it would attract customers back again to our shop.

S. Sure to. And then you might print your
ticket summut in the style of the real ones as
sold at the lottery-offices.

REFFS. Not a bad idea. It would look as if
we were somehow connected with the State
lottery itself.

MRS. R. And then issuing printed tickets has
such a respectable appearance.

REFFS. But, look here. Supposing that we
should get the prize, and have to pay the five
hundred pounds, could we not stipulate that the
amount should be taken out in groceries?

S. Won't do. People will rush at gold like
a bull at a red rag; but they won't stir for
treacle and mustard.

REFFS. But, again, why give five hundred
pounds? Would not two hundred and fifty
do? It's an enormous sum compared with
Hicks's beggarly twenty guineas.

S. No such thing! Yours is beggarly compared with his. His twenty guineas come out
of his own pocket. All that comes out of
yours is a few shillings for the sixteenth share.
His customers do get the chance of his money;

yours only get the chance of your chance. It's thousands to one that they never get nothing even to draw for.

REFFS. That's true enough; but, then, perhaps people won't be attracted to us by such a remote chance as that?

S. Yes, they will, cos people are fools. The sum's big, and that will make up for the chance being weak, if even they do think of that, and I dare say they won't.

REFFS. Well, really, I think that it is a very feasible plan. What do you say to it, my dear?

MRS. R. Yes; and very respectable, too. Only think! Five hundred pounds and real printed tickets. I wonder what those low people, the Hickses, will say to that? They will be terribly cut up, poor things. One almost pities them, with their paltry twenty guineas—pooh!

REFFS. Very well, then, we will decide on adopting this plan; and I think that we are entitled to great credit for hitting on it.

MRS. R. If it succeeds we'll call it Reffs's patent.

REFFS. I had my work to do to shape it out

of Shirty's rather crude notions. They required
to be unmuddled.

Mrs. R. Rough hints are very well, but they
want to be ironed smooth to get the creases
out.

Reffs. Still he did his best for us, poor
fellow! and if we find the scheme answer in a
week or two, he shall have a half-holiday, with
a half-crown to spend on it.

The scheme did answer; but all that Shirty
got by it was his half-holiday at Sadler's Wells
with me. His ingenious device was fathered
and mothered by Mr. and Mrs. Reffs, and he
obtained neither profit nor credit from it.

Sic vos non vobis
$\begin{cases} \text{build ye your nests, little birds !} \\ \text{grow ye your fleeces, O sheep !} \\ \text{gather ye honey, O bees !} \\ \text{draw ye, O oxen ! the plough.} \end{cases}$

So ends my friend Charley's little sketch,
which amused me at the time, and which I
introduce here with the less scruple, because
Shirty plays a rather important part in a
subsequent stage of these memoirs.

CHAPTER VI.

ON the day that I completed my twenty-first year, my uncle called me into his little study, and, placing in my hands a sealed packet, he said,—

"Frank, my dear boy, these papers were sent to me through a trusty friend by your father. I received them in 1725—fourteen years ago; and, in compliance with the directions in his hand-writing on the outside, I now hand them over to you."

I looked at the address, and found on it the following words:—"To be given to my son Francis Allerton, when he shall have attained the age of twenty-one. He may then peruse the contents. For my follies, my vices, and my misdeeds, let him make what allowance his

filial piety may suggest, and, by steering clear
of them, escape the fate of his unhappy father,
Andrew Allerton." I turned the packet
over and over mechanically, whilst a host of
conflicting emotions rose within me. I felt, by
a kind of intuition, that the revelations thus to
be made would be of a distressing nature, and
might prove subversive of the affectionate
veneration which I had always entertained
towards the memory of my father. Of my
parents I knew little, and that little I had,
from time to time, gleaned from my uncle and
aunt, whose kindly hearts had suppressed all
unfavourable details. I merely knew that my
mother had died in giving me birth; that my
father, who had suffered heavy losses through
connexion with the Jacobite rising in 1715,
had been finally ruined by an attempt to
retrieve his fortunes in 1720, by means of
speculations in the South Sea and other bubbles
of that epoch; and that he then returned to
Paris, where he died in 1725. Was I now to
know my father better only to respect him
less? Was I to be harrowed by a recital of
his " follies, vices, and misdeeds " ?

" Uncle," said I, while I felt my eyes

becoming dim with rising tears, "is it absolutely necessary that this packet should be opened at all?"

"If you regard it in the light of a duty, Frank," he replied, "you must not shrink from it."

"Why rend the veil," said I, "that time has thrown over past troubles and misfortunes? I seek your advice, my dear uncle, because you may be swayed by reasons unknown to me. For myself, I have little curiosity and much dread in regard to these disclosures."

"If," replied my uncle, "your father enjoins you to read his communication, you are bound to do so. But, let us see. No, there is no injunction. The words on the address are, 'He may then peruse the contents.' I think, therefore, that it is optional with you to open the packet or not."

"Thanks, uncle; then I think that I will decide on not disturbing the secrets of the grave."

"Follow your own inspirations, Frank. Besides, you can at any time unseal and peruse the communication, should you feel so inclined. It is not a case of 'now or never.' Take the packet. Lock it up, and you may make yourself acquainted with its contents whenever you feel more inclined than you appear to be now."

I thanked my uncle, and, acting on his advice, I locked the packet up in my private desk, where it remained for some years untouched. Under what circumstances I finally broke the seal will be explained later on.

This interview, and the subject of it, soon vanished from my memory, and I spent a happy evening with my kind guardians, who had invited a few friends to celebrate the occasion of my attaining my majority. Among them was Charley Frampton, who gave full vent to his high spirits, and amused us all by his playful wit, while, however, he shocked some (my aunt included) by the audacity of his satire. I could not help fervently hoping that time and experience might strengthen the wit, and temper the satire.

My life passed on very pleasantly. Most of the day was spent at the office, which I attended very regularly, and where I did my best to render myself useful. My evenings were mostly devoted to reading, and sometimes to music and chess with Alice. Now and then I escorted the ladies to a concert or to the opera, especially when the music was Handel's, for we were all great admirers of his compositions.

But the day of days to me was Saturday, for on that day I left the office early, and, unless the weather was very adverse, it became a settled practice that I should take Alice for a long walk each Saturday afternoon, "for the sake of healthful exercise," said the old ones, "for the sake of the exquisite enjoyment," thought the young ones.

Occasionally I would take what my uncle called a "bachelor's fling," and have a bout of fencing at De Livordy's; or take a dish of chocolate at the Cocoa Nut, to read the papers, and listen to coffee-house talk; or go with Charley to the play-house, where wit and licentiousness, splendid acting, and shameless ribaldry alternately charmed and disgusted me; or drop in at Figg's rooms to witness his wonderful adroitness at the foils, the gloves, and the quarter-staff.

One day I had only just returned from the office, when Charley Frampton rushed in with his usual impetuosity, saying,—

"Come along, Frank. I have had a tip from my dear, snuffy, old godmother in the shape of five bright golden guineas, and I want to drink her health."

"Why should I 'come along,'" said I, "merely because you want to drink your god-mother's health?"

"How can I drink it alone, silly boy? Look sharp! Don your walking-coat, thatch your head with your best triangular, assume your clouded cane, and I will give you a dinner at Pontack's."

"Who is he?"

"Pontack is not a 'he.' He was once, but he died forty years ago. Pontack now is a 'thing.'"

"What thing?"

"Blest ignorance! Only possible in a man who forms one of a strict, orderly, square, mathematical family like yours. Why, you're a regular barn fowl, that have got your wings so clipped to prevent you flying over the enclosure that you would hardly know a thing outside of your hen-coop but for such a friend as I am."

"Well, you have taught me much foolery,

Charley, I admit; but you have not yet told
me what 'thing' Pontack is."

"Well, get yourself ready," said Charley;
"tell your ladies that you are going into the
city with a demure Quaker friend, and I will
enlighten you as we walk."

I do as bidden, and we sally forth.

"Well, Frank," said Charley, "Pontack's is
a cook-shop."

"A cook-shop!" I exclaimed; "then why go
so far for one? I know of five close by, in
Holborn."

"A cook-shop it is; but it is the first in the
world. It caters for the wealthiest, the most
critical, and the most fastidious dinner-eaters
in London. Lucullus, Apicius, Vitellius, and
Heliogabalus feed there every day."

"Pretty company to introduce a friend to!"

"Peace, O tyro! Who has not dined at
Pontack's has never dined yet. To chew and
gorge is for brute animals; it is for man to eat
and taste. To these higher sensations of a
higher nature the culinary artists at Pontack's
worthily minister."

"Far-fetched apology for gormandizing!"

"Fie, beardless boy! If we are to satisfy

the animal cravings of nature, let us, at least, do it in the most intellectual manner. What is man but a complicated alimentary canal with trimmings, *videlicet* limbs, brains, and nerves? Now the very existence of the latter depends on the regularity with which the demands of the former are met. Pontack enables us to satisfy those demands with delight to ourselves, and so to combine duty with pleasure."

"And where is this temple of gluttony situated?"

"It is cosily ensconced near Christ Church, in a quiet passage leading out of Newgate Street, which is daily threaded by appreciative votaries. It is now nearly half a century since this celebrated establishment was founded by Monsieur de Pontac, Président du Parlement de Bordeaux (no less a person, if you please), who was a large vineyard proprietor. By means of this tavern he laid down a conduit for his wine, and so contrived that, while the barrel was fixed at Bordeaux, the tap opened in Newgate Street, London."

"Then Bacchus is the deity chiefly worshipped at this temple?"

"Not now: there are many other places

where you may get good wine; but exquisite
dishes, exquisitely served—the pure ideal of
gastronomy—nowhere but at Pontack's. No
abundance, mind! A profusion of food is
simply loathsome. No true epicure ever over-
eats himself. But you will get well-ordered
variety, and, in that variety, due proportion
and gradation. There must be harmony among
dishes as among colours. If ill assorted, one kills
the other, and artistic taste is cruelly offended.
No; drinking is here a secondary affair: to
hold the highest professorship in the science of
eating is the summit of Pontack's ambition." *

* It does not appear that the " proportion and gradation "
of dishes to which Mr. Frampton, Junior, refers, were of
universal recognition among the dinner-givers of that period.
Mrs. Delany (see her ' Letters,' vol. ii. p. 468) gives a dinner
to an archbishop, a bishop, and other notorieties, and takes such
pride in the *menu* which she has provided for the occasion,
that she describes it in full to her sister; and here it is.
After the FIRST COURSE, consisting of fish, soup, beefsteaks,
rabbits and onions, and fillet of veal, comes the

SECOND COURSE.
Turkey Pout,
Grilled Salmon, pickled Salmon,
Quails,
Peas, Cream, Mushrooms,
Apple-pie,
Crab, Leveret, Cheesecakes.

In similar talk we beguiled the time till we reached the ordinary, in praise of which my friend had been so eloquent.

We took the back road to the City, and almost repented it when we arrived at the purlieus of Smithfield; for in Cross Street we were all but crushed against the walls of the houses by a huge country waggon that occupied the whole width of the street, and we narrowly escaped being gored by a bull, driven to madness by the blows and yells of the cattle-men.

It was about five o'clock when we made our appearance at Pontack's. At that late hour the crush of business was over; the bulk of London had been dinnered, and had gone to vintners' and taverns to be wined. The spacious

---

This is followed by a dessert, just as promiscuous and incoherent, in which Dutch cheese comes next door to strawberries and cream, and orange butter follows currants and gooseberries. She gives another bill of fare at p. 331, and the following is the exact rotation of the first course :—Turkey, boiled leg of mutton, greens, soup, plum-pudding, roast loin of veal, and venison pasty. And yet Mrs. Delany had dined at Pontack's (as she herself states, p. 82), along with the Duke and Duchess of Portland, Lady Wallingford, and others, when they "took a jaunt to see city shows."—EDITOR.

room was dotted with only a few stragglers
like ourselves, so that we had an ample choice
of tables and attendants. A trim, active, well-
dressed waiter obsequiously received Charley's
orders. These he gave with a cool assumption
of familiar acquaintance with the latest in-
ventions of the culinary art—this *à la Bronsvic,*
that *à la Reine Caroline,* &c.—that extorted
my admiration. Of course they were quite
new and strange to him; but, to hear him, you
would fancy that he dined on French messes
every day. But on all subjects Charley had a
happy knack of making small acquirements go
a long way. This he effected by keeping out
of view, as much as possible, his immense stock
of ignorance, and displaying, as forcibly as he
could, his small stock of knowledge; just as
traders with limited stores parade the great
bulk of them in their shop-windows, while
dummies occupy the shelves inside.

Then came a learned conference on wines,
many of which, I am sure, Charley had never
even heard the names of, but which he flip-
pantly pooh-poohed, till at last the belligerent
powers came to a treaty, and contracted for a
bottle of *Pontac, haut cru,* to begin with.

While the dinner was being prepared, Charley opened a conversation with our attendant.

"Have you," he asked, "had much good company lately, Lewis? I believe your name is Lewis?"

"Beg pardon, sir; name's François."

Waiters are always so hurried that they get into the habit of lopping the pronouns off their verbs, and otherwise clipping the edges of their sentences.

"Ah, yes! François. Are you French?"

"Unfortunately, sir, English."

"Why unfortunately?"

"French waiter talking bad English gets three shillings a week more than English waiter talking bad French. Latter's my case, sir."

"Then why have a French name?"

"Allowed sixpence a week extra for that, sir."

"Hardly worth the money. I suppose you would black your face and wait as a nigger for another couple of shillings a week?"

"Certainly not, sir"; then, after a short pause, as though thinking whether we might be

inclined to embark in the speculation, he added,
"might for five."

"Too dear, François," said Charley. "Have
you had much good company lately?"

"Good, sir? Yes, sir; good for house,—not
for waiters."

"How is that?"

"People of quality, very grand, but very
stingy: much trouble, small returns. Prefer
serving open-hearted young gentlemen like
you, sir."

"But, you see, François, that your argument
proves too much: it makes it impossible for
us to be liberal without admitting ourselves to
be vulgar. To prove our gentility we shall be
compelled to be shabby."

"Oh, please; don't mean that. A lord
may be a stingy hunks; but don't follow that
every stingy hunks is a lord."

Dinner now interrupted this discussion. It
was no doubt a great work of art, and may have
been worth all it cost; but, before it was half
over, I had improvidently sated my appetite; so
that the last few courses formed charming pic-
tures for the eye, but had to be ignored by my
palate.

Towards the end of the symposium, when the grosser viands were about to be replaced by sparkling glasses and ethereal wine, Charley, glancing his eye round the room, suddenly exclaimed,—

"Ah! whom do I spy at that corner table near the window? Surely it is Harry Fielding!"

"Do you know him?"

"I have only met him once; but that is quite enough to identify that remarkable face."

"There are two of them at that table: which of the two do you mean?"

"Not the fat beast, with his back to us. How can that be a remarkable face? Why this fellow looks as if he had no face at all, but was a square block of body, with a hole on the top to bury half his wig in. Apoplexy has marked him for his own. No, not him; but the man with the keen, sharp features, who fronts us."

"The one with a very long nose?"

"Yes, and with an equally long chin."

"When that man is seventy his nose and his chin will meet."

"Then they will never meet, for he never will be seventy. He is living away at the rate

of three years in one. He is rapidly wasting
his fund of vitality. He is the wittiest and
giddiest of men. He writes plays by the
dozen, of which one or two are super-excellent
and the rest dull trash."

" Is he not the author of that exquisite burlesque, ' Tom Thumb ' ? "

" He is indeed ; and also of that awful rub-
bish, ' The Modern Husband.' He writes for
bread, and has no time to write for fame. He
has, I think—and so does my father, who is
keen on these matters—an immense fund of
original humour and wit ; and yet, such is his
hurry to produce a play, that, instead of
weaving his own materials, he pilfers other
people's, and some of his most popular pieces,
such as the ' Mock Doctor ' and ' Miser,' are
little better than translations from the French
of Molière."

" Perhaps," I suggested, " Duel or Morice *
press their spurs into his flanks, and urge him
into unhealthy activity."

" It is so, Frank, and more 's the pity. He
is of an excellent family ; but his father, the

* The " leading " bailiffs (Sheriff's officers) of that
period.

general, is poor, and the nominal 200*l.* a year
which he gets (or rather does not get) just
suffices to replenish his snuff-box. I have quite
a sympathy for poor Harry Fielding; for my
father allows me 200*l.* a year, with this great
difference, however, that he really does pay it."*

The general manager at Pontack's was a
naturalized Frenchman of the name of Baron.
He was a son of the celebrated French actor,
Michel Baron, well known as the chief performer in Molière's dramatic corps, and the intimate friend of the greatest dramatist that
France has ever produced. Pontack's Baron
(or as he was sometimes familiarly called, Baron
Pontack) was a man of about five-and-fifty,
well bred and well informed, who fulfilled the
duties of his station with shrewdness and
success. But it was on the topic of wines and

* This was written some years before Fielding had
immortalized his name by his great novel, 'Tom Jones.'
Mr. Frampton's prediction that his career would be a short
one was verified, as poor Fielding died in Lisbon at the age of
forty-eight. Had he lived, the world would no doubt have been
enriched by productions of great merit, for the only novel he
wrote subsequently to 'Tom Jones' (I mean 'Amelia')
exhibits to my mind a decided improvement on its pre-
decessor; although I know that this is not the general
opinion.—EDITOR.

vintages that he was pre-eminent. He had con-
centrated all his energies upon this one study,
and he was supposed to be the first judge of
bouquet in the world.

Charley had heard how fond Baron was of
expatiating on his favourite theme, and, as is
the frequent practice, he sent François with his
compliments, to invite him to share with us a
bottle of his best foaming Epernay. Mr. Baron
readily obeyed our summons, and we were soon
engaged in conversation. I could not but
admire the tact with which Charley, who had
never given the subject any serious attention,
conferred on his shallowness the appearance of
profundity by starting a theory which approached to a paradox. Nothing like a
paradox to simulate profundity. The novelty
startles, and the apparent absurdity provokes
attention. To have arrived at a conclusion
opposite to that commonly received necessarily
assumes that the speaker not only knows all
that other people can have to say on the subject, but a good deal more. It implies, though
it does not express, some such a course of
reasoning as this. "Of course the common
notion is so and so, on such and such grounds.

Everybody knows that; but if you go far
deeper than all that routine stuff, as I have
done, you will find the common notion quite
inconclusive, and you will agree with me that,
after all, it is quite within the limits of reasonable hypothesis that the old traditional suppo-
sition of the moon being made of green cheese
is not so far removed from the possibility of
truth as is vulgarly believed."

Charley boldly advanced a proposition that,
as he afterwards confessed to me, only occurred
to him on the spur of the moment.

"I have no doubt, Monsieur Baron," said he,
"that deeply as you have reflected on these
interesting subjects, you will agree with me,
who, with far more limited experience, have
also given them some thought, that the cultivation of the white grape-bearing vine is a mistake much to be regretted."

"In what sense, I pray you, do you conceive
that it is a mistake?"

"I mean that as a wine-producer the white-
fruited vine—the ' vitis vinifera fructu albo'—is
so much inferior to the purple-berried species, that
it ought to be extirpated and superseded by the
latter."

"This is quite new to me," said Baron; "pray explain yourself further."

"The true original natural vine," said Charley, as impressively as if he was sure of the fact, "bears purple fruit. The golden variety is a mere accidental sport. It is an unnatural monstrosity. White wine is an inferior essence. The sack of our ancestors, now called canary,—the Spanish Xerez, known as sherry,—the low order of wines, called Suresne,—all these sickly, yellow juices, are so infinitely inferior in flavour, in odour (or bouquet), in tone, and in colour to the noble produce of the purple grapes that they ought to give way to them, and all the best soils and slopes and sites now devoted to the former ought to be surrendered to the cultivation of the latter."

"Pardon me, sir," said Mr. Baron, with a deprecatory smile; "I have listened with attention to the views which you have so ingeniously propounded, but I regret that I cannot coincide with them. I cannot admit that the produce of the golden bunches is at all inferior to that of the purple fruit. I could find much to say on this subject; but I will confine myself to one instance. Till within the last sixty or

seventy years, the glorious vine districts of
sunny Champagne were planted with the purple-
fruited species only. The wine it produced
presented the same dark tint, delicate flavour,
and ambrosial perfume as do now the wines of
Gascony, which you mass together under the
name of claret, and of the large central zone
which you indiscriminately call Burgundy."

"And pray," triumphantly asked Charley,
"have you any fault to find with that delicious,
ruby-tinted produce?"

"Certainly not. I grant you, worthy sir,
that it was most highly valued, and, from the
chanoines of Rheims to the popes and cardinals
of Rome, it formed the special and favourite
beverage of ecclesiastical epicures. But a little
more than half a century ago, for reasons
which I have not been able clearly to ascertain,
the golden-graped vine became a general object
of culture in the vineyards of Champagne, to
the displacement of the old species, and white
instead of red wine became the staple of the
country."

"And I warrant me," put in Charley, tenta-
tively, "that it lost some of the celebrity which
it had formerly enjoyed."

" You are right, sir, it did, for a time; but .
soon, through the special interposition of Divine
Providence, a miraculous discovery was made
by a holy friar which added another to the
many blessings which man enjoys. About the
year 1700, Father Pérignon, a monk of the
Order of St. Benedict, supernaturally inspired,
invented a process which rendered the white
wine of Epernay and Rheims famous and
popular throughout the world. He made it
effervescent. Under his treatment it bubbled
and sparkled, and hissed and foamed, till the
spectators almost thought that it was the wine
itself that was intoxicated. Here was an immense addition to the sum of human pleasures!
This Pérignon wine (for so it was at first
named, after its inventor) realized enormous
prices. For a long time the secret was kept
inviolate, and effervescing champagne was a
luxury for princes. Since then the process
has become known to all wine-growers, the
price has fallen, and champagne has now
become almost vulgar, so extensive is its popu-
larity. Now mark! the effervescing process
has been applied with only very partial success
to red wines, and I therefore appeal to you

whether the sparkling golden nectar, which the plains of Champagne now supply, is not a striking improvement on the purple liquid which they formerly yielded. Honour, therefore, to the golden grape and its glorious juice!"

By this time we had finished our wine, and Charley, wishing to close the feast, merely answered,—

"You are a very eloquent advocate, Mr. Baron, and your cause had a powerful ally in the fitting illustration which this bottle afforded us of the excellence which white wine can attain. I regret that an appointment prevents me from arguing the point out with you to-day. *Au revoir!*"

In a short time, Charley having disembarrassed himself of some of his godmother's golden guineas, we departed, perhaps not much wiser, but certainly not sadder men.

We finished the evening by going to the King's Theatre, in the Haymarket, to hear Mr. Handel's new oratorio, 'Israel in Egypt.' It was brought out a few nights before, but had such poor success, and had been attended by such dwindling audiences, that to keep it "going" Handel had interspersed it with "favourite songs." These were horridly out of keeping, but they received more applause than any of the other parts.

I enjoyed the oratorio very well. There are in it some wonderful choruses, but they were badly sung, and by too few voices. They are so massive that to give them full effect they require a vast volume of sound, which they do not get from the limited vocal company which a theatre can afford to engage. When Handel first composed his oratorios, he intended them to be performed dramatically and in character, like operas; but as people objected to this, thinking it profane, he relinquished the idea, and now the oratorio occupies an equivocal and precarious position between an opera and a church-service. Indeed the oratorios of Handel are more fitted for a cathedral than for a play-house; and I cannot help fancying that they might create a profound impression if they were sung by numerous voices in Westminster Abbey, an event which however is not at all likely ever to take place.

CHAPTER VII.

THIS year is particularly impressed on my memory by the great frost which had set in at Christmas. The Thames was frozen over, and the navigation was not resumed till the 20th of February. Strange within what a limited range of temperature human life is possible! A few degrees make all the difference between our being frozen or broiled. Does all life then end above and below those narrow limits? Are such conditions as we know to be necessary to our own existence the only conditions under which any organized existence is possible? May there not be creatures to whom 500 degrees above, or 500 degrees below zero are the normal and healthy temperatures? I am inclined to think that there are. Forgive the passing speculation.

One day Charley called on me for a walk, promising that he would show me a curiosity. I acceded, and he dragged me right to the other end of that dreary and muddy thoroughfare, Tottenham Court Road, till he stopped opposite a stonemason's yard.

"Look now, Frank," said he; "does nothing strike you?"

I saw nothing but a lot of tombstones, cenotaphs, hic jacets, and square slabs ready to receive complimentary inscriptions from wealthy heirs to deceased virtues.

"You unobservant mole!" exclaimed Charley. "Look at this signboard. A tombstone rampant. Underneath, 'P. Whitehead, Stonemason'; and below that this delicious inscription, 'Si monumentum quæris, respice,' as much as to say, 'If you are in search of a monument, take a look round.'"

I was certainly much amused at this ingenious perversion of Sir Christopher Wren's celebrated epitaph into an invitation to inspect a stonecutter's stock; but it struck me that it was a long way to come for it, when Charley might have told me all about it sitting on a chair.

However, I quite forgave him, as on our way there and back he entertained me with a lively account of a dinner which his father had given two days before, and at which he had been one of the guests. I will give you my version of it, founded on Charley's narrative.

Mr. Frampton occupied a high and confidential post in the Secret Service Office, which brought him into frequent and familiar contact with the Prime Minister, Sir Robert Walpole. In common with all men of commanding talent, Sir Robert possessed the faculty of morally influencing all those with whom he came into contact. Some loved, some admired, some feared, and some hated him; but to none was he indifferent. Of those who hated him, by far the greatest number were actuated more by envy at his position than by personal antagonism to the man. On the other hand, those who loved him had the double incentive of regard for him individually, and of regard for his high office, which enabled him to shower down favours on his friends; and I need not say that he had many: what minister has not?

But among them he had none more zealous

or more faithful than Mr. Frampton. Walpole was his *beau idéal*, his idol; and he remained devoted to him through good report and evil report.

But it was not the Minister's public measures or his line of policy that Frampton defended or eulogized. He took it for granted that, emanating as they did from his chief, his measures were "all right." He did not trouble himself as to their intrinsic merits, nor did he perplex himself by reading what was said on the other side. If he lighted on an adverse article in the *Craftsman*, he simply cried "Rot!" and turned over to an account in the next column of a cock-fight. He loved Walpole for qualities which had their counterparts in his own nature. Both were clever, wily, sagacious, and good-humoured, but, at the same time, rough, imperious, overbearing, and unscrupulous; and both, without entertaining much admiration for, or indeed belief in, moral principle, detested and despised that spurious affectation of it which they deemed hypocrisy, and termed "humbug."

What excited Mr. Frampton's warm enthusiasm was Walpole's consummate dexterity in maintaining for so long a period his favour with the King and his majority in the Parliament. The humiliations which the Minister had to undergo to secure the former were little known to Mr. Frampton ; but, from the nature of his office, he was privy to the bribery and corruption by which the latter was obtained. Indeed, he was one of the main channels through which flowed the stream of seduction ; nor was the function at all uncongenial to his taste.

With an inconsistency, however, by no means unaccountable if analyzed, while he admired the giver he despised the receiver of the bribe. For the man who sold himself his contempt was unbounded ; but to the man who bought him he looked up with respect and admiration.

On the occasion of the dinner to which Charley had referred, the guests consisted of three of Mr. Frampton's colleagues in the Secret Service Office, and Charley was the only outsider, so that the conversation assumed quite a confidential turn. When the cloth was removed, and the servants, having replaced the edibles by the potables, had retired, the intercourse became more unrestrained.

Stragley, a young fellow who belonged to a

good old Whig family, was one of the guests. While thoroughly convinced that by serving his party he was serving his country, he entertained some foolish youthful crotchets (which were however vanishing year by year) as to the possible, though remote, contingency of patriotism not being incompatible with purity.

" Pity," he observed to Mr. Frampton, " that Sir Robert Walpole's ends, which are so laudable, cannot be attained without using means which are not—"

" You might as well say," replied Mr. Frampton, " that it is a pity you cannot rescue a drowning man without wetting your shoes. A Minister who should scruple at buying a vote to save his country would be a poor creature indeed."

" But the Minister who would contemn such devices, and rest his power on nobler foundations—"

" Would assuredly be turned out in a week —at least, in these times, gentlemen," continued Frampton, who, by this time, was far advanced in his second bottle, and was inspired both by his theme and his wine. " The only tests of the comparative efficacy of opposite means are success and failure. I decidedly prefer the strong man who wins the battle to the worthy man who loses it. Hence my admiration for Sir Robert. Battles are not won by the exercise of the cardinal virtues, but by hard blows and knocks. If you applaud the victor, you must not be sentimental about the blows and knocks. Friend Stragley extols Sir Robert's success, under which the country enjoys peace and prosperity, but would like him to achieve it by other expedients than those he uses : that is, he desires the end and shrinks from the means. Are you as competent a judge of the means of success as the man who has succeeded ? Sir Robert kills his man at fifty paces with his influence musket, and you tell him that he would have done as well with your purity popgun. Nonsense ! Let the strong man use the weapons which he knows to be best fitted to his purpose."

"Then," said Stragley, "for the men who owe their failures to the tenderness of their consciences you have no sympathy ?"

"None whatever," answered Frampton ; "not so much as the few drops that would make this bumper, which I toss off to Sir Robert's health, overflow. Such men are

like pistols loaded with bran instead of gunpowder, formidable to look at, but when they
are required to shoot the bran don't ignite.
Now Sir Robert is a pistol well charged with
real gunpowder, which never misses fire.
He is no sham, but a precious hard reality.
Those who have wrestled with him have found
that out. What he wants done he takes good
care to have done. When done, it is well
done; and if the means he used to get it done
were the surest means, then were they also the
best."

"But if state necessity justifies the men who
buy votes, what justifies the men who sell
them?"

"Nothing," warmly replied Frampton. "For
such men I entertain the most unmitigated contempt. They are either poor, weak creatures,
or wicked, unprincipled wretches. I have seen
lots of both classes; they have passed through
our hands in scores—scabby sheep or rapacious
wolves, every one of them."

"You are right, Mr. Frampton," said another
of the company—Mr. Wrigglesworth, a very
old hand in the office, and thoroughly inured to
the process of converting hollow enemies into

hollow friends; "they are a rum lot. The
poor ones do affect a kind of shamefaced reluctance at coming into the market to sell
themselves — a mincing air of 'My poverty
but not my will consents' resignation—but
those are the few. The great majority are im-
pelled by far lower motives than indigence,
such as, for instance, avarice, greedy to accu-
mulate; ambition, panting to rise, regardless
of the means; cowardice, fearing the shadow
of a danger; envy, grudging the position
which another has attained to; pride, grovel-
ling low in the dust, to stand high in the eyes
of the world; revenge, sinking all self-respect
in the longing to strike a blow at an enemy.
Such are the questionable objects which they
seek to attain by questionable means. The
healthy strain of open and honourable contention they feel unequal to. They are like sturdy
mendicants who, abjuring honest work, prefer
to beg."

"Bravo, Wrigglesworth!" said Mr. Frampton; "you know them well. But there is one
class that you have not referred to. I mean
the stately, high-flown men in buckram, who
are scandalized at the idea of taking money.

To sell their vote for gold! Out upon it! High-minded men!—are they to be confounded with the mercenary crew whose god is mammon? Perish the thought! At the same time, any honourable consideration—a red or blue ribbon, a post for themselves or their son, a piece of preferment, a deanery for a cousin, or even a place in the Excise for a poor relation, —oh, well, some of these things might induce them to reconsider their last vote, &c. In truth, my friend Stragley, if these are the people against whom you inveigh, I go heartily with you."

"Pardon the freedom of my remark, Mr. Frampton; but we are here among close friends. It is whispered in a certain circle of sound orthodox Whigs that Sir Robert is too lavish of his good things to those whose opposition he wishes to neutralize, which makes him too sparing of them to those whose support is his mainstay; that he is so profuse in his gifts to bribe his opponents, that there is little left with which to reward his friends; in short, that his partisans fare worse than his adversaries."

"Bah!" sneeringly retorted Mr. Frampton, "why what a fool Sir Robert would be to waste his favours on those who will support him, whether or no, when he can use those favours in securing the co-operation of those who would otherwise oppose him ! "

" Well, that is a consideration, certainly. But it savours more of policy than of gratitude ! "

" So it ought. What right has Sir Robert to indulge his own selfish feeling of gratitude to his adherents, at the expense of the general policy which is to promote the happiness of a nation ? The rewards that precede services that are to be rendered must naturally claim preference over those which follow services that have been rendered. But console yourselves, my friends, I do not think that there is any truth in the allegation. The national cow yields such an abundance of milk that there is plenty for all. Gentlemen, I will give you a toast. Here's continued health and endurance to the national cow ; and may her dugs never supply any but a Whig milk-pail ! "

The toast was drunk amid laughter and applause.

" As we are among friends," said Mr. Wrigglesworth, " and may therefore pick holes

in our party, allow me to say that instances
have occurred, more than once, in which the
votes have been given and the promised reward
withheld."

" As to that," observed Frampton, " served
them right."

" Perhaps so ; but it is bad policy. It injures
our credit in the market, and makes business
difficult.   I do not think that Walpole himself
ever committed such an error ; but I know that
it has occurred with his slippery colleague,
Lord F."

" Lord F. slippery !   Not a bit of it."
cried Frampton, who, though not caring a
button for Lord F., yet deemed it his duty to
uphold every person and every practice, every
man and every measure, connected with the
Walpole Ministry.   " I do not know anybody
that is more reliable than Lord F."

Loud cries of " Oh ! oh ! " greeted this
assertion, for Lord F. was notoriously as loose
in the performance of his promises as he was
obstinate in his adherence to his opinions.

" I maintain," continued Mr. Frampton,
" that no man can be more depended upon in
regard to both his opinions and his promises.

The former he never abandons; the latter he never keeps. In this course he is so consistent and unswerving that none can be ever deceived by him."

"Well, to be sure," replied Stragley, "in that sense you may be right. I understand that Shippen once said of Sir Robert—"

"That square-toed old Tory, Shippen! Pray do not quote the opinion of so bitter an opponent."

"An out-and-out Jacobite," added Wrigglesworth, "a rough bear, who thinks it manly to be rude, and calls acrimony candour!"

"Whom," continued Frampton, "Pope styles 'Downright Shippen,' because he could not say 'Upright Shippen' of such a rascal!"

"Be that as it may," rejoined Stragley, "what he said of Sir Robert was by no means ill natured. Speaking in his bluff manner, he said, 'Robin and I are honest men. He is for King George, and I am for King James. But as for those fellows with the long cravats, Sandys and the rest, they only desire places under one king or the other.'"

"Bravely spoken," said Frampton, "of the old fellow! But Sir Robert needs to have a few friendly enemies, for he has not a few hostile friends."

"Oh, I warrant," said Wrigglesworth, "that he holds his own against any of them, big or little. Talking of little, I remember, in 1733, when the proposed Excise Act raised such a storm in the country, Sir Robert was one night at the theatre in the Haymarket, and one of the comedians introduced in his part a disparaging allusion to the Excise Act. Sir Robert waited till the performance was over, then went behind the scenes and demanded of the prompter whether the offensive words were part of the play. Upon receiving an assurance that they were not, Sir Robert up with his cane, and gave the actor who had improvised them a sound thrashing for his impertinence."

All joined in approval of the Minister's spirited conduct; and the conversation then shifting into theatrical and other subjects Charley's report of it there terminated.

CHAPTER VIII.

THREE QUIET YEARS.   1741—1743.

DURING these years the current of my life
glided on so smoothly that it furnishes no
incidents worthy of being recorded. Nor was
the period enlivened by many stirring public
events.   The gradual defeat in Parliament and
final retirement from power of Sir Robert
Walpole occurred in February, 1742, and
formed a topic of universal interest.   For
twenty-one years he had occupied the post of
Prime Minister, and had been the most powerful man in the kingdom, not even excepting
the two kings whom he had successively served.
They were, indeed, kings ; but, as Shakespere
has it, he was " viceroy over them."   As plain
Sir Blue String (so he was called) he wielded
enormous power, while as Earl of Orford (which

he became after his fall) he is a mere cipher, and it is said even that he is in pecuniary difficulties from having spent too much on his huge house at Houghton. When he resigned, the king, hard and selfish as he is, instead of holding his hand for his kneeling servant to kiss, fell upon his neck, and, bursting into tears, affectionately embraced him. As at Alexander's death his kingdom lost its unity, and was divided among his generals, so after Walpole's fall the post of Prime Minister lost its power, and, while weak Wilmington occupied the post, the real power was distributed among the Pulteneys, Carterets, Newcastles, and others. It is said that no pope ever occupied the see of Rome so long as the twenty four years assigned to St. Peter. I doubt whether any Prime Minister will ever occupy the post so long as the twenty-one years that Walpole enjoyed it.

Although not fond of literature himself, he was the cause of much literature in others. He was a fruitful theme for prose and verse. He was alternately nauseously flattered and infamously libelled. Most writers began by praising him ; but when they found that he took

no notice of them, they tired of that, and
punished him, some by their silence, others by
their censure. Determined to get something
out of him, they first tried to wheedle him by
flattery, and, failing that, they tried to bully
him by satire. Sir Hanbury Williams is an
honourable exception. He was faithful to
Walpole from first to last. His witty poems
are the delight of the age, and he pelted the
Minister's enemies, especially Pulteney, with an
incessant shower of odes, burlesques, songs,
fables, and epigrams.

But with the common herd it was otherwise.
For instance, Harry Fielding, who, since we
met him at Pontack's two years ago, has taken
to a new field for his talents, and has just published the ' History and Adventures of Joseph
Andrews,' is an example of the grateful musk-
deer converted by neglect into the offensive
polecat.

By-the-bye, I may as well say that this ' History of Joseph Andrews,' which is amusing
enough, was written as a burlesque upon a dull,
prosy story called ' Pamela,' published by some
printer in Salisbury Court, which has obtained
a certain vogue lately.

Well, to go on; Fielding in 1730 wrote some verses to Walpole, in which he unblushingly asks him for a place. He winds up by saying,—

> " If you should ask what pleases best ?
> To get the most, and do the least.
> What fitted for ? You know, I'm sure,
> I'm fittest for—a sinecure ! "

Getting no response from the careless Minister, he took his revenge by lashing him with lampoons.

Dean Swift, the most perfidious of flatterers, and the most acrid of satirists, attacked him vehemently. As long as political antagonism was the sole motive for the onslaught, the abuse was mild; but a trifling matter of a private nature supervened which fired the Dean's fury into a flame, and the invective became coarse, bitter, and personal. A young relation of the Dean's whose name resembled his (for the young man was christened Deane Swift), but whose character did not, for he was neither witty nor wicked, was known to and patronized by Sir Robert Walpole. The Minister had taken a fancy to the young fellow, and urged him to take orders, adding that, if he did so, he would provide for him, and, perhaps, in due time make him a bishop.

This reached the ears of the Dean, who was equally enraged with his namesake and with the Minister. His hopes of becoming a bishop himself had long since vanished, and the idea of a younger man and a relation being promoted over his head was intolerable. He bullied Mr. D. Swift, whose estate was mortgaged to the Dean for 1,500*l.*, into a promise that he would not enter into the Church at all, and thus had the pleasure of depriving his relative of all his chances of advancement.

On Walpole, he took the only revenge which it was in his power to take, and levelled at him a bitter and caustic satire. Some idea of it may be formed by the following extract:—

> " With favour and fortune fastidiously blest,
>   He's loud in his laugh, and he's coarse in his jest."

(Who was so " coarse in his jest " as the Dean himself ?)

> " Oppressing true merit, exalting the base,
>   And selling his country to purchase his place.
>   Of virtue and worth by profession a jiber ;
>   Of juries and senates the bully and briber."

The terseness of the invective hardly atones for its excessive virulence.

Talking of terseness, a friend of mine, who knew him well, gave me the following concise description of that able writer but unsuccessful statesman, Lord Bolingbroke. "A tall, fair man, pitted with the small-pox; vivacious, witty, passionate, good-humoured; a sad libertine; drinks hard, sleeps little; indefatigable, a hearty friend, a bitter enemy."

About this time cousin Alice and I began to take great delight in the examination and study of flowers and shrubs and trees, and in our Saturday-afternoon walks paid frequent visits to the physic-garden at Chelsea, under the able direction of Mr. Miller, to Bishop Compton's plantations at Fulham Palace, and to Mr. Peter Collinson's fine collection at Peckham. We also made an occasional inspection of Mr. Gray's nurseries at Fulham, celebrated for new American plants, of which a catalogue has lately been published.*

What an infinite diversity there is in nature!

* This famous old nursery-garden still survives; and its reputation is well maintained by its present owners, Messrs. Osborne & Sons.—EDITOR.

For instance, of the Iris (Floure-de-luce) old Gerarde describes no less than twenty-nine species. Now his big folio was published in 1636, a century ago, since which time a great number of new species have been introduced from abroad by Tradescant, Collinson, and others.

I wonder whether the time will ever come when every plant or tree growing throughout the world in temperate zones, having a climate similar to ours, will be introduced and made to grow in our English gardens and plantations. Why not?

By-the-bye, what an elaborate work that is of old Gerarde's. It contains no less than 5,000 woodcuts of a large size; being pictorial representations of the different shrubs, &c., which he describes. One is confused and oppressed by the immense number of plants which he records, and of which he sings the praises. Each of these, if we are to believe the venerable enthusiast, possesses an average of five different curative virtues; so that, if our "physitions," as Gerarde spells the word, do not remove all our various ailments, it is certainly not Gerarde's fault. For gout and rheumatism alone he enumerates no less than 400 infallible specifics; so that if man is still subject to those complaints, it is due to sheer wanton neglect. Indeed, if there be a tithe of truth in the sanative properties of these various herbs, why should not pain and disease be altogether eliminated from the face of the earth? "Cur moriatur homo, cui salvia crescit in horto?"

Unfortunately I have noticed that the number of "infallible remedies" is always large in proportion to the incurableness of the malady; just as the stronger the fortress is the more troops are required to besiege it; with this difference, however, that the troops combine for a simultaneous attack, whereas the remedies have to attack the disease one by one. For, to mix the 400 specifics for rheumatism together in one huge bowl, and administer that, would, I fear, be of little avail.

CHAPTER IX.

ONE evening, in the spring of this year 1744, I returned home rather late from the office, and found assembled the usual cosy family group. My uncle was deep in the perusal of that bitter and ferocious attack of Milton's on poor old Salmasius that literally slaughtered him. My aunt was engaged in conning over a more innocent but still tougher work, viz., Lord Clarendon's answer to Hobbes's 'Leviathan.' I did once try (being strenuously enjoined to do so) to read that work, but I stuck fast at one particular sentence, about the middle of the book, which was spun out to the unconscionable length of one page and a half quarto, without a full-stop. It was a most wonderful sentence, perfectly grammatical, and logically congruous, but so swollen out by parenthesis within parenthesis, so cut up into subsidiary statements loosely cemented to the general framework by "if," "as," "but," and other copulative conjunctions, that you had to examine how it was that the eleventh separate proposition dovetailed into, and was connected with, the ten preceding ones, before you could understand the sense of the whole. For twenty minutes I toiled at this monster sentence,—I laboriously made it out,—shut the book, and never opened it again.

But to return: my aunt was reading, or trying to read, that interesting book, and dear cousin Alice (how sweet the smile with which she welcomed me home!) was embroidering some stiff piece of brocade.

Soon after I had joined the circle my uncle said to me, "Frank, we have had a visitor here to-day. Read this." I took the document which he handed me. It was in the form of a large square-folded letter, addressed as follows in a stiff, formal hand:—

"For my worthy and estimable kinsman,
    "MEREDITH UPPENHAM, Gentleman,
"These, by the hands of my young and singular good friend,
    "MASTER MARTIN BREREWOOD."

Inside was a letter of introduction and recommendation from a distant cousin of my uncle's in favour of the said Martin Brerewood. From the crabbed characters and the old-fashioned style of superscription long since discarded, I at once knew that the sender must be that venerable piece of antiquity, Sir John Newsom.

We all of us, and so did the world at large, entertained respect for the character, and derived amusement from the harmless foibles, of this worthy old man. He was a Jacobite member of the House of Commons, but was popular with all parties. Sir John adored the past, and used all his efforts to prevent the present from running away from it. All old customs, old modes of thought, and old reputations were the objects of his panegyric. It was more from this peculiar bent of mind that he retained his loyalty to the Stuart exiles than from any deep conviction of the abstract justice of their cause. Indeed, in the exhibition of his political predilections he was so mild and courtly—they assumed so much more the semblance of an archæological hobby than of party feeling—that the Whigs bore him no malice; and, in fact, from his genial manners he had become a kind of personal pet in the House, even among the Walpolites.

I glanced over the letter, and then asked, "Pray, uncle, did Sir John's 'young and singular friend' favour you with a call?"

"He did, Frank," returned my uncle. "He delivered his credentials personally this morning."

"Some homespun provincial, I suppose, sir," said I, "anxious to see the Tower, and sup at Vauxhall?"

"No such novice as you think, fair nephew," replied my uncle. "You Londoners fancy that all country people must be clodhoppers, just as the Greeks held all non-Greeks to be barbarians. But, as to that, ask your aunt and Alice. Women are critical judges in regard to rusticity and good-breeding."

"Has this Mr.—Mr. Brerewood," asked I, "been introduced, then, to the ladies?"

"Yes," replied my uncle. "After half an hour's converse with him in the little study on matters of some importance, I invited him into the withdrawing-room, where, in accordance with a message I had sent her, your aunt had prepared some slight refreshment."

"And what, dear aunt," I asked, "is your verdict on this representative of the shires of England?"

"Nay," replied she, "you should rather say of the shores of France; for he is just from there. He is a great traveller, and Paris appears to be more familiar to him than London."

"Then I suppose," said I, with a faint approach to a sneer, for I somehow had taken a dislike to this intruder, "he has brought over the newest French fashions, and is duly stored with French frippery and affectation?"

"Not at all," replied my aunt: "he appears to be a thorough gentleman, of good address and pleasing manners. Of his moral principles I of course cannot speak, but I was gratified to learn that he is warmly attached to the good old cause."

"Perhaps," insinuated I, "he had ascertained your leaning towards it, and to obtain your favour he may have affected a sympathy—"

"Which he did not feel, you mean," interrupted my uncle. "You do him injustice, Frank. I have good reason to know that he is not only zealous, but actively engaged on

behalf of the rightful monarch. His is no
mere lip-service."

"Would, Frank," exclaimed my aunt, "that
you were half as warm an adherent to the
cause of the Stuarts as he is! You seem to
me to be growing more and more indifferent to
it every day."

"But, dear mother," kindly interposed
Alice, "Frank never dealt largely in professions."

"It may be well," replied my aunt, "not to
be too forward, but to keep back altogether is
quite a different thing. What a falling off
from his poor father, who sealed his devotion
and loyalty by ruin and death!"

"Come, my dear aunt," said I, "you must
admit that the fact of my father's ruin and
death being the result of his connexion with
the party can hardly constitute its title to my
favour."

"Why not?" she replied. "The daughter of
a soldier does not love her country a whit the
less because her father died in its defence."

"True, my dear," said my uncle; "but the
dulce et decorum does not repair the bereave-
ment, or wipe away the tears. At the same

time I do wish that Frank were more eager and
cordial in the adoption of the hereditary
political doctrines of his family."

"But, sir," said I, "may not those doctrines
be susceptible of modification from changes in
the circumstances on which they were originally
based?"

Modestly expressed as were my doubts, they
startled my aunt, and she exclaimed,—

"Frank, I am surprised! Why, this reasoning is the very essence of Whig sophistry! It
is the ignoble plea of expediency itself."

"Modification, do you say?" added my
uncle. "I do not believe in modification. It
gradually unfastens, nail by nail, and screw by
screw, the entire framework of the political
fabric. Octavius Cæsar modified the old Roman
constitution, and it lapsed into Imperialism.
William of Normandy modified our old Saxon
polity, and it lapsed into feudalism. William
of Holland modified our old Church and State
organization, and it lapsed into—"

"Yes," broke in my aunt, impetuously,
"into Whiggery, infidelity, Hanoverian wars,
German bad women, foreign mercenaries, heavy
taxes, a national debt, a corrupt parliament—"

"Well," interrupted my uncle, "let us say, et cætera, et cætera. To tell the truth, I would rather hark back to the old cover than move on to beat up new ones. Be that as it may, I fancy, Frank, that your great friend, your *fidus Achates*, young Frampton, has mainly contributed to unsettle your notions. Now, when I introduce you to Mr. Brerewood, I hope that you will take to each other, and he may then perhaps buttress you up on the other side, and get you upright again."

"Well, uncle," I replied, "I pity the man who requires buttressing on both sides to make him stand erect. However, I shall be happy to make the acquaintance of your hero."

"Very well, Frank. I have invited him to dine with us next Thursday at four o'clock; and mind you get away from your office early enough to join us."

"With pleasure," I replied. "Aunty dear, bear with my political scepticism for the present. I am giving, and shall give, the question serious study and reflection, so as to arrive at some definite and fixed opinion upon it."

"Pray do so, Frank, earnestly and searchingly."

" But what," asked I, really anxious to know the penalty I might have to pay for political heresy, "if the result of my search be convictions different from your own ? "

"Heaven forbid, Frank! I can scarcely think that honest inquiry can lead you astray. But, even if it should, better that than your present cold indifference to matters that vitally affect the welfare of your country."

" May we not say," put in Alice, modestly, " that the community is like a picnic, to which, as all enjoy it, each should bring some contribution, however small,—except children, such as Frank and myself."

No immediate rejoinder being made, she quickly added, so as to change the rather ticklish conversation, " And now, Frank, if you will bring out the chessboard, I will show you a wonderful checkmate given by Count Bruhl to that fierce antagonist of mine, Anna Rollston. She showed it to me to-day."

" That square-headed spinster is, I fear, a better player than either you or I."

" She is," replied Alice; " and that is why I felt a little malicious pleasure in seeing how thoroughly the count demolished her."

" That, however, is not very much to her discredit, for I suppose that he is the finest player not only in England, but perhaps in Europe."

" I thought so too, but — you remember Danican, the composer of that little French song you liked so much, ' Je t'aimerai toujours,' the young fellow who at eleven years of age wrote that motet for four voices that Louis XV. praised so highly ? "

" Well, yes : what of him ? "

" Miss Rollston tells me that he is a first-rate chess-player, and that when Count Bruhl, some little time ago, visited Paris, he was beaten by young Danican."

" That is singular, for now I think of it, I was told at Parsloe's that there was only one man who could beat Count Bruhl, and that was a Frenchman named Philidor. Are there two Frenchmen, then, to whom the count must yield the palm at chess ? "

" Not at all," replied Alice ; " they are one and the same man. He was born Danican, and dubbed himself Philidor; probably a travelling name, as kings on a voyage, to preserve their incognito, call themselves Duke or Baron So-and-So."

"Bravo, then, Monsieur Danican-Philidor! By-the-bye, Alice, we shall have a chance of seeing him, for I am told that he intends visiting England next year."

"You must get an introduction to him, Frank."

"I will; and in the mean time you must sing me 'Je t'aimerai toujours' (what pretty words they are !), in honour of Danican, and after that we will have a game at .chess in honour of Philidor."

"Very well; but I am thinking that Philidor had better remain Danican, and concentrate his energies on musical composition, as that may hand his fame down to posterity, whereas of immortality as a chess-player, there is no possible chance, and his talent for the game will only live in the remembrance of the few personal friends with whom he may play."

I fully acquiesced in this opinion, and so another quiet and happy evening passed away.

CHAPTER X.

On the following Thursday I was duly introduced to Mr. Martin Brerewood. As he has played an important part in the most eventful crisis of my career, I must present to you the most life-like picture of the man that I can draw.

At the time of his introduction to our circle he was about thirty years of age. He was very tall, and his graceful figure was so well proportioned that no one would have imagined that he measured, as he did, fully six feet in height, till he was in immediate proximity with other men; and then, such was his erect carriage and imposing mien, that his stature appeared greater than it really was. The features of his face, taken separately, might hardly perhaps challenge rigorous criticism. His mouth was a little too deeply set between

lips just a little too thin. His nose was somewhat too abruptly aquiline, his chin a trifle too
long and projecting, and his complexion too
uniformly pale and colourless; but these deviations from the ideal were very slight, and the
tout ensemble was very handsome and fasci-
nating. It was a face that impressed all
beholders, men as well as women, with an irre-
sistible sense of manly beauty and mental
power. But it was his large hazel-brown eyes
which perhaps formed his most powerful
charm. As your own eyes encountered their
bright beams, you felt as though he were looking through and through you. They seemed
to dive into your inmost soul's recesses, and you
could not help returning involuntary glances
as though of welcome and reciprocity. It was
curious, however, to notice that in his eyes yours
could read nothing. Penetrating but impene-
trable, they searched you, but refused to be
searched. You might yield up to them the
secret of your own feelings, but you could
elicit no revelation in return. Indeed, I never
knew him to abide a steady gaze from others;
when prolonged, his own eyes sank and lowered
under its influence.

His smile was enchanting ; for every feature, especially his radiant eyes, seemed to smile in unison with his lips ; and yet there were times when you could not but fancy that this sun-lit smile broke out too suddenly, and was too suddenly quenched—as though it were an act of volition not of impulse. His exuberant dark-brown hair, combed away from his ample forehead, hung in graceful curls over his shoulders ; for he used powder sparingly, and only where the hat crowned the head. When I add to all this that he always dressed well (I mean as a gentleman, not as a fop), and that his manner and address were as attractive as his figure, you have as complete a sketch as I am competent to give you of Martin Brerewood's external appearance.

As to the man himself, the inner being, of which only the husk or shell has been described, I must decline any attempt to portray him. I must relinquish in despair the task of analyzing that busy brain and wayward heart. His actions, as I narrate them, his motives, as I unfold them, will best guide you to an estimate of his character.

His natural abilities were of the highest

order, and an excellent college education had afforded them full development. Long intercourse with the best society, abroad as well as at home, had added to the native graces of a well-bred English gentleman that ease of manner, and adaptability to the tastes and humours of others, of which it is so difficult to resist the charm. His courage and skill in the use of the rapier had been tested in more than one duello, and he was unanimously pronounced by the ladies to be of unrivalled elegance as a performer in the graceful minuet or lively coranto.

He was the second son of Eustace Brerewood of Briarwood, the representative of an old Devonshire family, to whom the estate had descended from a long line of ancestors. The Briarwood estate, from which the family name, with a slight deflection, was derived, was not a very large or valuable one, but was amply sufficient to entitle its possessors to rank with the landed gentry of the county, and to enable them to maintain a good position among their compeers. The traditions of the family had for generations been connected with the High Church and State party. Martin's grandfather

had served against the Duke of Monmouth at
Sedgemoor in 1685, and had feasted the ruthless Jeffreys at Briarwood, on his savage circuit
through the western counties. Eustace Brerewood, Martin's father, had been one of the
plotters, and nearly one of the actors, in the
abortive outbreak of 1715. Nurtured in these
hereditary principles, it is no wonder that
Martin Brerewood should have thrown himself,
with the vigour and energy natural to him, into
the vortex of that desperate struggle which the
adherents of the Stuarts were organizing in
1743 and 1744, and which came to its climax in
1745.

Such was the man whose fate, for a brief but
eventful period, was so intertwined with my
own that it seemed as if we could not deviate
into separate paths. At every step I took, he
was in my way, as I in his. When first we
met, we were, at least I know that I was, disposed to cultivate friendly relations. There
were many points about him which excited not
my envy, but my admiration ; and I sought not
to copy him, but to improve myself in those
matters in which I felt his superiority. Our
interests, however, soon clashed, and, as you

will see in the sequel, I had to sustain his powerful enmity. You must confess that he was a formidable antagonist to encounter.

My uncle's party was but a small one. The only guests were Mr. Brerewood, Sir John Newsom, his introducer, and Alice's late governess and old friend Miss Rollston, a lady who occupied an undefined position in that large, shifting zone of years that separates youth from old age. During dinner little passed that was noticeable. Mr. Brerewood was very polite and attentive to the ladies. Alice received his compliments quietly; but I observed that my aunt was by no means insensible to the desire he evinced of being agreeable to her, and she was evidently pleased with him.

When the ladies retired, the conversation gradually assumed a political turn. My loyalty, which of course meant disloyalty to the reigning government, was taken for granted, and the usual Jacobite toasts were drunk. "Worthy Mr. Uppenham," said Sir John, "it has delighted me to be the means of introducing to you such a fine chip of a good old block as my young friend here."

"I am grateful to you," replied my uncle,

" for the acquaintance. The Brerewoods of Briarwood are well known to me by name and fame. They belong to the good old stock—the *prisca gens mortalium*—who have made England what she is. They have staunchly adhered—"

" To the good old cause," broke in Sir John, who had a knack of finishing sentences for his friends whenever they halted at all in search of a word; " yes, you may well say that. My old friend Eustace, the father of your young guest, was up, and very nearly out, in 1715; and his grandfather fought against Monmouth. Now we see their merits reflected in Master Martin."

" I fear, Sir John," said Brerewood, " that your compliment to me is premature. I have done nothing yet, and the praise due to my ancestors it is not for me to claim."

" Modestly spoken," said my uncle. " ' Quæ non fecimus ipsi vix ea nostra voco.' "

" But I would fain hope," continued Brerewood, " that the time is not far distant when the old soldiers in the fight will don their armour, and the younger ones may then show themselves not unworthy of their sires."

" As to the old ones donning their armour,"

observed Sir John, "I presume you speak metaphorically; for these aged bones of mine require gentle treatment, which they do not always meet with at the hands of mine ancient foe, the gout."

"Of course, my dear Sir John," replied Brerewood, "I spoke metaphorically. Your part is to contribute good counsel, moral influence, and able guidance. It is for such as Mr. Francis and myself to supply the thews and sinews."

"Ah, well, yes; no doubt," said my uncle, hesitatingly. "All in good time; but at present we are far off from a crisis; and mean time—"

"Mean time," interposed Sir John, "what we have to do is to carefully watch events."

"Pardon me, respected sirs," rejoined Brerewood, glancing round the room to make sure of our being alone, and lowering his voice, "events are hastening on, and the sincerity of every man's professions will, ere long, be fairly tested. I presume that we are all firm and devoted friends here?"

I was not at all prepared to become the confidant of, far less a participator in, any political

design or measure in favour of either of the
contending parties. My convictions as to
"under which king" I was content to live
were as yet unformed, so that, till I had de-
liberately arrived at a conclusion, it was premature to "speak or die!" and I wished to
avoid committing myself. I therefore ventured
to reply, "If that question only refers to the
private regard and friendship which we entertain towards each other, I am sure that we
shall all answer it in the affirmative. But if it
implies our common concurrence in some project connected with public affairs or political
parties, I am hardly prepared to go so far."

"I am not aware," said my uncle, "of any
special project having been mooted."

"Nor I," said Sir John. "I entertain
decided opinions, sincere wishes, and, I may
add, strong hopes; but as to a practical project,
that is quite a different thing."

"It will be my privilege, as well as my
duty, gentlemen," said Brerewood, "to lay
before you at an early date some definite plan.
Meanwhile, it would be a pleasure to me to be
made quite sure that we all of us entertain the
same ulterior views. I fancied that Mr. Aller-

ton's remark might possibly bear a construction at variance with such an accord."

"May I venture to suggest," said I, "that this is hardly the time or the place to enter on explanations and discussions on matters so delicate?"

Neither my uncle nor Sir John Newsom were at all anxious to elicit Brerewood's "definite plan." Like many other of the Jacobites, especially the elderly ones, they faithfully clung to their abstract theory; but, when it came to carry it out in practice, their enthusiasm somewhat cooled. As Sir John had said, they warmly entertained opinions, wishes, and even hopes, but it was not so easy to screw them up to the point of staking life and property on their realization. My suggestion, therefore, met my uncle's approval, and he said, "Well, perhaps Frank is right. You see, Mr. Brerewood, we might be interrupted, if not overheard, and it might be as well to—"

"Yes; adjourn the meeting," interposed Sir John. "I admire our friend Master Martin's ardour; it is quite refreshing in this age of apathy and scepticism to be carried back to the good old times of earnestness and vigour, when

men fought and bled for their party, and the
sword cut the Gordian knot which, nowadays,
it is sought to unravel by intrigue and cunning.
But we must not compromise the good old
cause by hasty and indiscreet proceedings.
By-the-bye, Uppenham, you remember the
grey mare that you admired so much; I
have sold her to Lord Carteret for thirty
guineas!"

"Have you, really?" returned my uncle;
"and very cheap, too," &c.

Brerewood felt that this abrupt change in the
conversation was an unmistakable protest
against its continuance, and, gracefully accept-
ing the position, though not without a smile in
which a trace of contempt was discernible, he
turned to me and said, "Are you fond of music,
Mr. Allerton?"

"I am, very," I replied, "and from your
question, Mr. Brerewood, I infer that you are
no less so."

"You are right. I intend to-morrow night
to go to the King's Theatre, to hear Lampugnani's new opera, 'Alceste.' If you are not
better engaged, will you do me the favour to
come and take a dish of chocolate with me at

the Cocoa Nut, and afterwards accompany me
to the theatre?"

"I accept your invitation with pleasure. At
the same time I must confess to you that, in
my opinion, Lampugnani does not, as a composer, stand in the highest rank."

"Well, I like him," returned Brerewood.
"However, you cannot have heard his 'Alceste'
yet, for it is only just out. I understand that
Monticelli sings divinely in it, and that the aria
'Questo bacio' is a masterpiece of elegance
and pathos. Before you finally condemn poor
Lampugnani, you must listen to this air."

"I will cheerfully give your favourite another
trial; but as a rule," I said, "I consider the
Italian school rather light and flimsy, and prefer the massive style of Bach and Handel."

"Ah, yes. Handel, or rather, Hendel, if
you please! A heavy German, ostentatiously
patronized by the Hanoverian clique. Our party
does not take to him. We put his music down
as noisy and eccentric. Too many notes!"

"Is there not," I asked, "a little political
bias in that judgment?"

"Frankly, yes, a great deal. But, hang it!
one must not surrender to the enemy even in

the matter of crotchets and quavers. We 'honest men' must be true to each other; so long live Bononcini, even though—"

The company now broke up at the suggestion of Sir John, and we joined the ladies upstairs. Mr. Brerewood made himself very agreeable. He gave us some pleasant sketches of Parisian society, and related some racy anecdotes of Lord Bolingbroke, with whom he was intimate, and whom he had lately seen in the French capital. Alice afterwards sang a couple of songs in her usual charming and impressive manner, and our guest was evidently much struck with her performance.

Before departing, Mr. Brerewood persuaded the ladies to make up a party to Vauxhall on the following Tuesday, but as my uncle never cared for such gaieties, I was deputed to act as his representative, and the ladies were to be escorted by Mr. Brerewood and myself. Somehow I did not altogether relish the footing of quasi-intimacy into which that gentleman was drifting, but I had neither the power nor the right to interfere.

After the ladies had retired for the night, my uncle said to me, "Look here, Frank, you

will have to make up your mind decidedly as
to your politics. I am bound, partly by conviction, and partly by old associations, to the
cause of the Stuart family. The latter influence
you also must feel, for loyalty is traditional
in your family; but how far it may be coun-
teracted in your case by other considerations I
cannot tell."

"To say the truth, uncle," I pleaded, "I
have never yet devoted serious thought to
political subjects."

"Time then that you should. Under a form
of Government that is definitely settled the
necessity is not so cogent. But these are dis-
jointed times, and every man should contribute
his push either to one side or the other."

"I have never had the presumption to
imagine that anything I could say or do could
exercise the slightest influence over the course
of events, so I even let it flow on."

"It is the duty of every citizen to contribute
his mite, if not to the conduct of public affairs,
at least to the formation of public opinion. 'Of
what avail is my single mite?' you will ask.
Of great avail. The accumulated force of
millions of these individually small mites is pro-

digious. You hardly realize the enormous
aggregate power of minute things in immense
numbers. A drop of water is a mere atom,
but out of myriads of these drops is built up
the wave that dashes the frigate against the
rocks; a single locust is an insignificant insect,
but a large swarm obscures the sky and re-
duces a province to famine; the carcase of a
tiger is, in one day, picked clean to the bones
by a single colony of ants; and it is by the
adaptation of the same principle that our rapacious Ministry has been enabled last year to
extract from the nation the incredible sum of
ten millions of golden guineas. No; believe
me, Frank, it is not only a mistake but a
wrong for any man to withhold his mite, whether
in thought, or word or act, especially at so
critical a period as is the present."

"You allude, no doubt," said I, impressed
by my uncle's earnestness, "to the efforts which
are likely to be made to change the dynasty?"

"Say rather to restore the dynasty. It is
the Whigs who made the change. Yes; a
struggle is impending. I view it with evil
forebodings, and not without some apprehen-
sions of danger to our Protestant establishment

from the advent of a Catholic king. Nevertheless, my path lies distinctly defined before
me, and I must follow it. But you?"

"I do not see my way so clearly, but I
promise you, uncle, that I will seek earnestly
for light on this matter; and I acknowledge
the necessity for a decision in respect to it."

"Very good, Frank, I hold you to your
promise. I can make allowance for your hesi-
tation while you are weighing the *pros* and
cons,—while the suit is *sub judice;* but you
must remember that your aunt feels more than
she reasons on the subject; and therefore so
magnifies the *pros,* and so parvifies the *cons,*
that you must expect far less allowance from
her."

"Does not the question, sir, resolve itself
into this? Under which dynasty can good
government and the welfare of the people best
be secured?"

"No; it goes deeper than that. Yours is
only the particular question; whereas you have
to examine the general question to which the
former is subsidiary. The present King George
—the usurper—may (we will suppose it, though
far from true) be a better ruler than the present

King James, the rightful monarch; but that is a mere accident. The next King James may be a better ruler than the next King George, and then what will you do? Will you change back again? No; you must disentangle yourself from special and exceptional cases, and grapple with the broad, general principle which we contend for. It is that of direct hereditary succession. We maintain that, putting aside the disputed theory of Divine right, hereditary succession is a clear and well-defined principle, which should not, and shall not, be departed from. In fact, unless it be adhered to strictly and thoroughly, it ceases to be a principle, and becomes an expedient. It ceases to be a standard for men to conform to, but becomes a regulation for men to make or unmake. That principle unerringly points out the man who is to be monarch of these realms. Depart from that, and who is to appoint the man? Some will be for Dick, some for Tom, and some for Harry; and civil broils and perhaps civil war must ensue. You are wafted to and fro, *arbitrio populous auræ*. The monarchy virtually becomes elective, like that of Poland, and, I fear, with the same disastrous results."

"But are there not," I asked, "exceptional cases, in which a departure from your principle would be productive of more good than an adherence to it?"

"The same question might be asked as to occasional deviations from truth. No doubt there are exceptional cases in which a departure from truth would be productive of more good than an adherence to it."

"Yes; but a violation of truth involves a general evil out of all proportion to the particular advantage it may, in isolated instances, secure."

"That is just what we say of the direct hereditary principle. And now, Frank, I will say good-night. I do not want to force my views upon you; but I do ask you to give them fair play, and to consider them carefully and dispassionately."

I readily promised my excellent uncle that I should do so, and we separated for the night.

CHAPTER XI.

A DECLARATION.

ONE glorious afternoon in May (it was on Saturday, the 15th—I remember it well) Alice and I were taking one of our wonted country walks, and had seated ourselves to rest on a moss-clad knob formed by the clustering and knotted roots of an old ash-tree. For years past, ever since we were children, we had been accustomed to take such walks. At first they were enjoined on us by my uncle and aunt for the sake of exercise and health; but we soon took such delight in these pleasant rambles that they had long since ceased to be a duty, and had become a treat and a luxury. Saturday was the day that we generally selected for our stroll, as on that day I returned rather earlier from the office.

We were both of us passionately fond of wild flowers, and we gradually learned the names and special abodes of all the rarer beauties. We ascertained and noted the particular spots which each species affected, and watched over the growth and welfare of our favourites as though we had ourselves planted them. Indeed, we did try our best to transfer them to our own little plot of ground in London, but in vain. Like caged wild birds, they sickened, pined, and died. The more we nursed and petted them the less they thrived. So that, as they refused to dwell with us, we had to visit them in their own native haunts, and a source of never-failing delight it was.

We found a patch of swamp in one of the lower parts of Hampstead Heath, skirting a small pool, which was the dwelling of the insect-trapping sun-dew,* with its hairy leaves, each hair exuding a dewdrop; of the spreading bog-pimpernel,† buried under its own

---

* *Drosera rotundifolia.* I give here the botanical names, as they are now known, of the plants named by Mr. Allerton, as the English names do not, in all parts of the country, refer to the same plant.

† *Anagallis tenella.*

swarm of pink flowers; of the modest, succulent water-blinks;* of the scorpion-grass,† whose flowers shade off from yellow to blue during their short span of life; of the venomous rascal crow's foot,‡ creative of beggars' sores, with several other bibulous water-plants.

Then we had discovered, "few and far between," two or three waste, sheep-trodden knolls, whose short, fine herbage was intermixed with wild thyme,§ grateful for being trampled on, and emitting most fragrance when most crushed; bird's foot,‖ with its minute, three-clawed fruit; heath bed-straw,¶ hugging the ground in long tresses, powdered over by myriads of snowy flowers; buck's horn plantain,** whose skeleton leaves starred the soil with horizontal tufts; the wiry milkwort,†† whose crested blossoms are arrayed now in purple, now in pink, and now in white; and other diminutive creeping-plants whose dwarfish growth eluded the teeth of the browsing cattle.

---

* *Montia fontana.*
† *Myosotis versicolor.*
‡ *Ranunculus sceleratus.*
§ *Thymus serpyllum.*

‖ *Ornithopus perpusillus.*
¶ *Galium saxatile.*
** *Plantago coronopus.*
†† *Polygala vulgaris.*

There was a favourite old crumbling wall in Islington that divided the road from a farmstead. This was a mine of wealth to us. Besides an abundant and varied crop of mosses and liverworts, it yielded to us the trailing thread-stemmed toad-flax,* never bare of flowers, the wall pennywort,† whose juicy leaf sits centrally on its stalk, like a mushroom; those dainty ferns, the hairy-backed ceterach,‡ the mortar-loving wall-rue,§ and the black-stalked spleenwort,‖ while the summit was crowded with the crimson snapdragon,¶ the fragrant wallflower,** the shining crane's-bill,†† whose lower leaves seem stained with blood, and other gay flowers.

We knew of a little sunny, reclining nook, wherein revelled the wild strawberry,‡‡ with its sweet fruit so tantalizingly small, the shy and retiring Moschatell,§§ the luxuriant golden bed-straw,‖‖ and the bristling bugloss.¶¶ We had

---

* *Linaria cymbalaria.* ** *Cheiranthus cheiri.*
† *Cotyledon umbilicus.* †† *Geranium lucidum.*
‡ *Ceterach officinarum.* ‡‡ *Fragaria vesca.*
§ *Asplenium Ruta muraria.* §§ *Adoxa moschatellina.*
‖ *Asplenium Adiantum nigrum.* ‖‖ *Galium verum.*
¶ *Antirrhinum majus.* ¶¶ *Echium vulgare.*

exultingly discovered a little trickling brook, issuing from some shale through which a road had been cut, whose mouth was bearded over with a spongy tuft of golden saxifrage,* and whose bed was for some distance lined with ivy-leaved bell-flower.† In short, we had a score of stations for our various vegetable pets, to each of which in turn we paid loving visits.

But, to resume. We were seated, Alice and I, in one of those fields near Highgate which skirt Swayne Lane, and before us lay the glorious expanse of London town, with its hundred steeples presided over by the noble dome of St. Paul's.

Up to this day no word of love had ever passed between us. Like brother and sister we had grown up in daily tightening bonds of sympathy and affection. Never had a cloud darkened our companionship. We each felt, we neither doubted, the sincerity of our mutual regard. But it had as yet no distinctive character. The genial warmth of our cousinly attachment glowed equally from day to day, month to month, year to year, without being fanned into the fierce flame of lovers' love. I

* *Chrysoplenium oppositifolium.*   † *Campanula hederacea.*

had never had occasion to gauge the depth of my feeling towards Alice. We had always lived together without hindrance and without check. We had never looked into the possible future. As was yesterday, as is to-day, why should not to-morrow be? Where the stream of existence flows in smooth, unbroken continuity our modes of thought may undergo change, but the change is so gradual as to be imperceptible. It requires some break, some sudden shock, to crystallize the old habitual into a new conscious state of being. Some such process had occurred with me within the last few days, and had opened my eyes to the true nature of my feelings towards Alice.

It was Martin Brerewood's attentions to her that aroused me. What did this man mean by showing his admiration for Alice? Did he dare to propose to himself to stand between me and her? Had not my life hitherto been bound up with hers? Could I tolerate the notion that the time might come, perhaps was coming, when we should no longer walk hand-in-hand along the road of life? Oh, no, no!—perish the thought! And yet I had done nothing to ensure my possession of her. I had simply taken

for granted that no one would interfere between us.

But now a chill of uncertainty benumbed
me. What, if Alice, loving me only as a dear
brother, should prefer another to love as a
husband? What if my uncle and aunt, looking upon me only as an adopted son, should
have other views as to the selection of a son-in-
law? Fool that I had been to have left this
vital matter so long in doubt! To have waited
until another suitor put forth his claims before
I put forth mine! To be, as it were, second in
the field! I now felt the full, glowing fervour
of man's love for woman. Newly awakened
hopes and fears thrilled through my soul, and I
determined, without delay, to know the worst
or the best.

We had agreed to take our accustomed walk
on the Saturday I have referred to, and that
was the occasion I had fixed upon to ascertain
my fate. During our walk, I must have
appeared to Alice very dull; for, easy as the
task of speaking my thoughts appeared till I
attempted it, the moment I opened my mouth
to commence I stammered, hesitated, and suddenly turned off to some trivial remark. My

heart beat violently, my mouth was parched, and a nervous tremor ran through my frame. Do not laugh at me, ye who read this. If you do, it must be because you never had so large a sum of happiness trembling in the balance. A misplaced word, an equivocal phrase, too much ardour or too much coldness,—in fact, the slightest mistake, I nervously and absurdly feared, might, perchance, be misconstrued, and mar the happiness of a life.

We had been for some little time gazing silently at the sun-lit prospect around, when, seized by a sudden impulse, I took Alice's hand in mine, as I had often done before, but never with the same feeling and significance, and, looking at her fondly, I said,—

" Alice, we have been very happy, have we not ? "

" Very happy, Frank," she replied ; " everybody is so good to us."

" Let us, then," I suddenly exclaimed, " swear to be happy all our lives ! "

" Silly youth ! as if swearing eternal happiness would give it us, or insure us immunity from troubles."

" At all events, if they came, we could bear

them all the better if we bore them together. With you, dearest Alice, at my side, I could ' smile at grief'; without you—but what am I saying? I could not live without you."

" Do not put it so strongly, Frank. A fever, an accident, the duties of life—many things may part us, whether we like it or not."

" The duties of life?" I exclaimed, almost fiercely. "What duties? Surely you cannot mean that there are duties that could step between us?"

"I know of none at present, Frank," she slowly said, " but I can imagine."

"Stop, Alice," I exclaimed fervently; "it must come out! Kindly hear me! I love you, dearest, with an intensity of love compared with which our old childish and cousinly affection is as cold as ice! This no longer suffices me. No! I myself feel infinitely more,—I want infinitely more from you. Alice, will you be my wife? Nothing less than a wife's love can satisfy me." And, as there was no instant reply, I added in alarm, "Have I been too abrupt, too rash, too presuming?"

As I poured out these almost incoherent phrases, I looked searchingly at Alice. Her eyes were cast down, her face was roseate with blushes, and for a few moments she remained motionless as a statue. Suddenly she lifted her eyes to mine (I observed that they were moistened, but not quite overflowing with tears), and, presenting me her hand, she said, gently but firmly,—

" Frank, I will be your wife ! "

O magic words that filled my soul with unutterable joy ! How in rapturous terms I thanked her, how we interchanged sweet confessions, how we unveiled our hearts to each other, how she reclined her head on my breast, how I snatched the first passionate kiss of love, —all this I need not describe. What a contrast to my feelings a few minutes before ! Then I was a prey to fears and doubts, faintly tempered by bashful hopes ; now my heart was swimming in bliss.

How long we remained on that rugged seat of gnarled ash-roots I never knew. It seemed like a few minutes, but it was impossible that we could have said so much, felt so much, and lived so much in that short space of time. Besides, the shadows had singularly lengthened, and the sun had made sensible approaches towards the horizon, so that, unless the earth had been revolving on its axis with suddenly accelerated velocity, we must have tarried in that happy spot for a considerable space of time.

At length we set out homewards. Our conversation gradually descended from the empyrean heights of romance to the dull level of reality.

"In all these dreams of happiness," said Alice, "we have taken for granted, Frank, that my choice will meet with the approval of my father and mother."

"Can we doubt it, dearest? They have reared us together as playmates, and they have left us to enjoy each other's company as man and woman. They must have foreseen our attachment, and probably we are now only dutifully carrying out their own designs."

"Certainly it is reasonable to suppose that my mother would otherwise have warned me against you, sir. But perhaps she underrated your attractions, and did not think you dangerous."

"But your father, Alice, must have known that *you* were, and ought to have cautioned me in good time. As he has not done so, he has wickedly exposed me to peril, and must take the consequences."

" On the other hand, it is strange that nothing has ever been said by my mother, in reference to me and you, denoting any views as to our future relations to each other. It is true that her strong mind is not given to dwell on such matters. But, Frank, we must not remain in this false position a moment longer than necessary. You will take the earliest opportunity of speaking to my father, as I shall of confiding all to my mother."

" Be it so, dear girl. But supposing—well, supposing " (and here an aguish feeling again began to creep over me) " that there were some opposition, surely—"

" Dear Frank," said she, " suppose nothing at present. Let us turn to brighter thoughts. I fancy—well, was it not a rather sudden impulse that led you to your welcome folly of this afternoon? Yesterday you were still a mild cousin ; to-day you are transformed into a brisk lover."

" You quick-sighted sylph ! The transformation was not quite as abrupt as you have stated, but still—"

"And shall I tell you who hastened the catastrophe? It was Mr. Brerewood"; and she looked at me with a knowing smile.

"Again you are right," I replied, somewhat sheepishly.

"His attentions, disagreeable as they were to me, were still more disagreeable to you, as I gladly noticed."

"The presumptuous coxcomb! To imagine that with a few honeyed phrases and empty smiles he could jauntily win away from me a treasure to which it had taken me a lifetime to deserve the slightest claim!"

"It is not always, indeed, not often that such a dreadfully long process is required to kindle a flame. Poets tell us of love at first sight. However, I think, Frank, that you are too hard on Mr. Brerewood. He may not have known of your pretensions to my hand. Indeed, I myself could only make a guess at them."

"Surely, Alice, you must have observed how much I loved you?"

"A woman is not justified in trusting in these matters to observation. She expects to be spoken to as well as looked at. The eye may be eloquent, but her 'Yes' or 'No' must be uttered only in reply to the tongue."

"I am sure Brerewood noticed my feelings towards you, just as I noticed his evident admiration."

"Which made you jealous, and your jealousy made you speak out. Thus, as I said, I am indebted for your declaration to Mr. Brerewood."

"But, Alice, you must admit that if his admiration was evident to you, mine must have been, to say the least, quite as much so."

"Not at all," she replied. "His admiration was clearly for the woman, while yours might have been only for the old playmate and cousin. Indeed, you confess that it is only recently that the nature and purpose of your admiration became evident to yourself. It was not for me to forestall you in the discovery."

"True, Alice, I loved you all along with the same kind of love, but did not know it. The fact is that I had been trotting by your side for so many years that I required a slight touch of the spur to break out into a canter."

"But you see now, Frank," she said, with a winsome smile, "that just as I could not reject

Mr. Brerewood before he made an offer, so I could not accept you before you proposed, sir."

" Well," said I, exultingly, " at all events now, darling, I have proposed and you have accepted, and I am the happiest of men."

By this time we had reached home.

CHAPTER XII.

On the morning of that happy Saturday which had given me the sweet assurance of Alice's love, a long conference had been held between my uncle and aunt and Martin Brerewood. I was then of course at the office, and Alice had been designedly sent out by her mother to execute some commissions and make some purchases, which necessitated her absence for a couple of hours. Neither of us was, therefore, aware that a meeting had taken place. It was only in after years that I learned from my uncle the particulars which I will insert in this place, to which they chronologically belong. I must be pardoned if I describe what passed in a conversational form; for while, not having been present, I may put in each speaker's mouth words different from those he really used, and

may perhaps change the order in which the
subjects discussed were actually presented, I
can vouch for the general accuracy of my
description, not only as to the topics adverted
to and the results arrived at, but also as to the
mode in which they were viewed and treated
by each interlocutor.

MARTIN BREREWOOD. " Before I enter on the
details which I have engaged to-day to give
you, should you persist in your intentions,
forgive me if I remind you in a formal manner,
first, that the design with which you are about
to be identified is, however praiseworthy;
not unattended with danger; secondly, that
your participation in it is spontaneous, and is
not due to any persuasion used by me; and,
thirdly, that you have not yet committed
yourselves, so that you are still in time to draw
back, if you so choose."

MRS. UPPENHAM. " Thanks, Master Martin,
for your consideration; but we should hardly
have gone so far as we have already gone,
without having duly reflected on the risks
involved in the enterprise; and as to your
share in the formation of our resolve, make
your mind easy, for we have arrived at it not

out of regard for you, but from a deep conviction of the sacredness of the cause, and from a
feeling of devoted loyalty to our rightful
sovereign King James the Third."

Mr. U. "I presume also, friend Brerewood,
that our concurrence in a common cause does
not bind us irretrievably to opinions from
which we may dissent, or to proceedings of
which we may disapprove?"

M. B. "Most decidedly not, my dear sir.
It was only a stern sense of duty that overcame
my reluctance to utter a warning that might
seem to convey a doubt of your earnestness.
But I have performed that ungracious task, and
now beg to turn to a more congenial topic.
To free our country from a detested usurpation
is the end which we all have in view, and
I invoke your aid and co-operation."

Mrs. U. "Our ready willingness to assist we
have already signified in general terms, and
to ascertain in what particular shape our
assistance is required was the professed object
of our meeting to-day."

M. B. "Quite so, madam, and I will explain.
The unfortunate issue of the expedition attempted last February has rendered it necessary

to weave afresh the web which that disastrous event destroyed."

Mrs. U. "Many of our friends here have been led to doubt the sincerity of our French allies on that occasion, as well as the rumoured extent of their preparations."

M. B. "They do injustice to the French Government. A well-appointed army of 15,000 men was assembled at Calais, Boulogne, and Dunkirk, commanded by the greatest general of the age, Marshal Saxe; transports were collected and constructed to convey them to the shores of Kent, with an ample supply of arms, ammunition, siege-trains, &c., and Prince Charles himself superintended the preparations, and was to be escorted to his dominions by this formidable array. Could France be expected to do more?"

Mrs. U. "Certainly not, Mr. Brerewood. The loyalists in England only asked for 10,000 men as a nucleus round which to rally. They would themselves do the rest, and that little army would soon have swelled into ten times its number had it landed. But it did not land."

M. B. "But was that the fault of France?"

Mrs. U. " That is the question which we wish to have clearly solved. We know that the French squadron that was to convoy the transports with troops to our coasts was attacked and driven back by Sir John Norris's fleet; and that so far the French had to yield, and English prowess, exerted in a bad cause, was victorious. But the French ships were only dispersed, and not destroyed nor even injured; and some are sceptical as to the real cause that led to the sudden and total abandonment of the enterprise. A destructive storm was alleged. Was that only a pretext, or was it a reality ? "

M. B. " My dear lady, it was a terrible reality. It was one of the most furious tornadoes that ever swept over the northern shores of France. Of the larger ships several were totally wrecked, and the smaller vessels and transports were so dashed one against the other that few escaped injury. The loss of life was fearful, and all hopes of conveying the troops across the Channel on that occasion vanished. Alas! it was a sad reality, and no pretext. It seemed as if, for some inscrutable reason, Providence had decreed that the expedition should not take place at that juncture."

'Mr. U. "England is lucky in storms. The same mysterious intervention saved her from the Spanish Armada. The designs of men may be based on the firmest foundation of known causes and effects, but out of the infinite unknown there is suddenly launched a thunderbolt which shivers them into dust. Beware of the unexpected; it is generally calamitous! Nor does the worthiness of its purpose protect a design from such evil chances. *Nec fortuna probat causas, sequiturque merentes.*"

Mrs. U. "I thank you, Mr. Brerewood, for your explanation. It is complete and satisfactory. I thought it right to place before you in their strongest light the misgivings as to French sincerity which some have entertained, or at least expressed, in order to elicit your opinion of them. I am glad to see that they are far from being shared by you."

M. B. "Far indeed, madam. And I hope that you also are now free from all doubt, as part of my mission is to claim renewed confidence in French support."

Mr. U. "Hard fate! That England should

be unable to right herself without French aid !
—that we should have countrymen for foes, and
enemies for friends ! "

M. B. " Yet it is so. I am in communication
with most of King James's adherents of any
note. With barely an exception, they pro-
nounce it folly to rise unless supported by
foreign troops. With an army, however small,
as a rallying point, with the presence in their
midst of the chivalrous prince, Charles Edward,
to represent his father, success would be certain ; the bold would rush forward with alacrity,
the wavering and timid would, *non passibus
æquis* perhaps, but in due time, follow, till all
England was roused from the lethargy which
makes Hanoverian rule possible, and we should
have the revolution of 1688 enacted over again,
only with the parts reversed."

Mrs. U. "Have you found our friends zealous
and determined ?　Are they numerous and influential ? "

M. B. " Zealous to enthusiasm, madam, and
determined unto rashness ; always, however,
under the condition that the assistance of foreign
troops shall render it not positively imprudent
for them openly to display that zeal and deter-

mination. As to their numbers, if you include those who silently and covertly wish well to the cause of the Stuarts, and whom a gleam of success would rally round their banner, you may compute them at three-fourths of the population; but if you refer to those who are prepared to take a bold initiative, and to lead instead of following, the muster-roll is a fair but more limited one."

Mr. U. "How can you expect a larger proportion of political than of religious martyrs? We are a Protestant people, but it is under the condition (to use your phrase) that our lives and fortunes are not to be jeopardized by our creed. Witness our marching backwards and forwards between Popery and Protestantism at the beck of Henry VIII. and his two daughters!"

M. B. "To increase the number of our active friends, to marshal them into a compact and united body, and to direct their energies towards a defined and practical end, such is my mission from your sovereign and his ally, the French king."

Mrs. U. "Say then, Mr. Brerewood, what is it that you wish us to do?"

M. B. (*producing a paper.*) " To sign this document; but first let me explain further. You know that the most powerful Minister in the French government is the Cardinal Tencin, who owed his promotion to the Cardinalate to the influence of our King James III. with the court of Rome. His gratitude for this friendly act, as well as the dictates of policy, induced the cardinal to organize the expedition of which we have been lamenting the failure, and which, had it been attended with success, would by this time have freed England from foreign domination. As our friends will not (and I am far from censuring their prudence) take action without French co-operation, our object now is to prevail on the cardinal to renew his efforts, and to repair the failure of last February by making a fresh and vigorous attempt to land an army in England, with Prince Charles at its head."

Mrs. U. " And will he do so ? "

M. B. " He will ; and the more boldly, as he has not the same motive for reserve as in February; for then war had not been declared between France and England. Now, however, it is different : war was declared in March, and hostilities have commenced. The English Ministry, to humour their master's Hanoverian proclivities, are directing all their efforts to the war in Germany, and England is almost denuded of troops, so that a more favourable opportunity for our operations could not present itself."

Mrs. U. " Is then the French Government actually concerting the measures on behalf of the king to which you have alluded ? "

M. B. " Not yet; and that brings me to the point to which I am to call your attention. When the last abortive attempt was planned, the cardinal had (with few exceptions) only verbal assurances, indirectly conveyed from a number of gentlemen of position, ability, and wealth, that as soon as the standard of James III. was unfurled in Kent, under the auspices of a French force, they, and through their influence crowds of others, would flock to it. Their sincerity was unfortunately not put to the test; but the French Government now require, before it engages in so serious an undertaking as the invasion (so to call it) of England, to have the written (instead of as before the verbal) assurances of the king's adherents that they will, the moment the French army has disembarked, rise in arms, proclaim King James, join the French, and take an active part in the struggle."

MRS. U. "That demand does not seem an unreasonable one. I presume that the paper you hold is the document to the required effect, and you wish Mr. Uppenham's signature to be attached to it."

M. B. "You are right, madam, it is so; but I still have a few words of previous explanation to offer. You will only find some fifteen or sixteen signatures to the memorandum, and for this paucity of names there are several reasons. In the first place, I have not yet called on one-half of the persons who are down on the list furnished to me. Then a large proportion of the most influential as well as the most zealous of our supporters have, in the exercise of an option offered them, preferred signifying their adhesion to the engagements contained in this paper in separate direct letters addressed to the king. Of these letters some have been confided to me for delivery, and others have been sent directly through other channels. This option is of course also submitted to Mr. Uppenham, and it is for him to make his election. Again (and this category includes the largest number), many have signified their willingness to add their names to the paper as soon as a certain number of signatures have been obtained to it. Some stipulate for twenty, others thirty, and several fifty; so that I am in this dilemma, that as long as signatures are really valuable I get but few, but the moment I shall have obtained the necessary number (and fifty will answer every purpose) they will be forthcoming in superfluous abundance."

Mr. U. " The silly flock will not follow three sheep over the stile, but they will six."

Mrs. U. " The faint hearts! As if, supposing them to be men of honourable intent, and sincere in the cause, it could matter a straw which name appeared first and which last! Indeed, the contention ought to have been for the earliest place in the list."

M. B. " Bravely spoken, Mrs. Uppenham! Would that such earnestness and courage as yours were more frequent among those with whom I have to deal! I assure you that I am sometimes moved to wrath, and sometimes chilled into discouragement, by the difficulties which I have to encounter."

Mrs. U. "I can imagine that your task is no easy one."

M. B. "No, indeed! I have to encourage the timid, animate the cold, stimulate the lazy, embolden the cowardly, arouse the hesitating, flatter the conceited, cajole the mercenary, and in each case to be on my guard against the treacherous. No; my task is no easy one, but I am sustained by the hope of success and my devotion to the cause."

Mrs. U. "Mr. Brerewood, I admire your energy. Your services deserve the grateful recognition of every loyal subject. I believe, Meredith, that I may ask Mr. Brerewood to hand you the paper for your signature?"

Mr. U. "Certainly; it is not that my name is of itself of much importance, but its value may be a little enhanced by its being among the earlier signatures. *Bis qui cito.*"

M. B. "Many thanks for your unhesitating compliance. And now there is another request I have to make in furtherance of the cause which we have at heart. May I venture to express it?"

Mrs. U. "How can you doubt it? We have now entered into a solemn engagement to serve

His Majesty and to assist in the restoration of his rights, and you will find us ready to put our hands to the work."

M. B. "'There are three waverers of somewhat high position, whom I am anxious to bring under a written agreement. Each promises to sign provided the other two will, but not one of them will take the initiative; nor will they, though they occasionally meet in society, consent to a meeting at each other's houses, nor at my lodgings, nor, indeed, at any place to which any suspicion might attach. But, from what dropped from one of them, I have reason to believe that they might attend a rendezvous under your roof. If you would kindly spare one of your rooms for an hour, some day next week, it might be the occasion of securing some valuable recruits to His Majesty's service."

Mr. U. (*returning the paper, after having signed it*). "I see nothing in this document which any loyal subject of James III. could hesitate to put his name to. Do I know any of the three gentlemen you allude to?"

M. B. "Two of them you know personally, and the other one by reputation. But I have passed my word to two of them that I shall divulge their names to no one until they have definitively joined, or declined joining. The third, who has not bound me by such a promise, is Mr. Gayley, a cousin of the late Mr. Shippen."

Mr. U. " Would my presence be required ? "

M. B. " It would not be objected to, if such were your wish; but I question whether it would assist me, as such shy birds are more easily approached by a solitary sportsman. Indeed, if I were able to assure them that you would be out of town on that day—"

Mrs. U. " I understand. It is rather humiliating that any friends to the king should require such manœuvring; but I suppose we must take men as we find them, and if you will let us know the day fixed for the meeting, I will select it for a visit to the Broughtons, at Chigwell, and I have no doubt, Meredith, that you will accompany me."

Mr. U. " Certainly, my dear. I will take care, Mr. Brerewood, that a room shall be placed at your disposal on that day."

M. B. " Many thanks; and I shall hope to give you a good report of the meeting. Meanwhile, there is one more topic which I should like to broach, if you will not think it too great a liberty."

Mr. U. " Speak freely, pray."

M. B. " I have the greatest personal regard for your nephew Mr. Allerton, but I have reason to believe that he by no means shares our political opinions."

Mrs. U. " I fear that you are right; but have you any grounds for supposing that he is not only indifferent, but hostile, to them ? "

M. B. " Frankly, I have ; and I strongly advise you not to let him know one syllable of the engagement Mr. Uppenham has entered into, or, indeed, anything of what has passed between us to-day."

Mr. U. " Frank is perfectly aware of our feelings of devoted loyalty to the king. He promised me some days ago to institute a thorough inquiry into the great question of the day, ' Who is our rightful king ? ' and to let me know the result. I shall this evening call upon him to give me his reply."

M. B. " I trust that his decision will be in favour of King James, and that we may find in him a trusty ally."

Mrs. U. "I reluctantly confess that I doubt it. Frank's mind has been inoculated with Whig venom, administered by that conceited young man, Frampton."

M. B. "Do you mean the son of that man in the Secret Service Office, who for many years, formerly under that clever knave Walpole, now under that knavish dullard Pelham, has been the impure channel through which those infamous bribes were conveyed which have perverted the morals, corrupted the honesty, and effected the apostasy of so many men who otherwise would have remained faithful to the good old cause?"

Mrs. U. "The very man! He fully deserves your invective."

M. B. "A political Satan, whose mission it is to tempt the weak to violate their consciences and forswear their convictions! to whom truth and loyalty are as evils to be extirpated, and Whiggism and Atheism as virtues to be fostered! whose gifts are as fatal as the shirt of Nessus, and whose very touch is contamination! Strange that the hard-earned gold of honest Englishmen should be used to extinguish English honesty!"

Mrs. U. " I share your just indignation. It is the son of this man that Frank Allerton has chosen for his intimate friend."

M. B. " I have heard of this young man, too. Specious, flippant, and cynical, he is an amusing but dangerous companion. He is devoid of religious principle ; and his writings— for he is a literary hack in pay of the Government—are full of bitter sarcasms and malignant sneers directed against our holy cause."

Mr. U. " And yet, in what intercourse I have had with young Mr. Frampton, I never noticed any tendency towards cynicism, or heard any remark savouring of either irreligion or of the other extreme, intolerance."

Mrs. U. " Naturally he would play the hypocrite before you, and so add one more to his other vices."

M. B. " That young Frampton is in close communication with the Government I know for certainty. In what capacity I only know from rumour."

Mrs. U. " And what does rumour say ? "

M. B. " That he collects intelligence, chiefly personal, and reports it to his employers."

Mr. U. " In other words, that he is a spy.

It may be, but I should hardly think so. Even
if true, we must fancy him base to the lowest
depths of degradation to suspect that he would
make use of his intimacy with Frank to extract
from him information as to what was passing in
this house."

M. B. " I have too little knowledge of the
rules and etiquette of that vocation to determine
the exact point at which the spy ends and the
friend begins; but the open, truthful nature of
Mr. Allerton must be completely at the mercy
of an artful and unscrupulous man."

Mrs. U. " If Frank declares his determina-
tion to side with us, I will trust him implicitly.
If, on the other hand, he pronounces in favour
of the present order of things, there may be
danger to our plans in his constant proximity,
and we shall have to seek a remedy."

M. B. " By-the-bye, Mr. Allerton and I
have an appointment this evening, and I am to
call here to fetch him. I have promised to introduce him to some friends of mine. If you
will now excuse me, I will take my leave."

The conference then ended, and Mr. Brerewood departed.

CHAPTER XIII.

THE COUNTESS MOLINA.

A FEW days before the eventful Saturday which I have described, Martin Brerewood paid a visit to his co-partner in political intrigue, the Countess Molina. As I and my destiny were deeply involved in the arrangements made by them at this interview, I will give a sketch of it from memoranda which fell into my hands a long time afterwards.

The Countess Molina had arrived from Genoa two or three months previously, with letters of introduction from high-class people there to a few families of good position in London. She rented handsomely furnished apartments in Clarges Street, appeared possessed of ample means, and received the visits of many reputable people. But it was soon evident that, for some reason or other, her lady friends were

falling off, and by degrees the bulk of her
visitors became composed of influential gentlemen of the Jacobite party. Although coming
from Italy, and bearing an Italian name, she
spoke Italian indifferently, but French with
great fluency, which she explained by stating
that she had been educated and had spent most
of her life in France. She also talked English
with some ease, but, as is usual with foreigners,
selecting the wrong words, placing them in the
wrong order, giving them the wrong pronuncia-
tion, and bestowing an excess of emphasis on
the wrong syllable of the wrong word.

She was a fine portly woman of about fifty,
with a dark complexion, dark hair, and black
flashing eyes, of a commanding presence, gifted
with a voice so melodious that it gave a charm
to every solecism she uttered. She was dressed
in the newest, which by no means always
implies the most extravagant, style of fashion.
For instance, the widest circumference of her
hoop was not at the lowest part of her dress,
as was the prevailing mode, but higher up
towards the hips, though not so high up as the
stiff farthingales of the Elizabethan epoch, so
that the dress fell in almost perpendicular folds

down to the ground, instead of expanding
gradually from the waist and reaching its
greatest amplitude at its lowest extremity. This
rational modification of the monstrous hoop
which, in a room where an equal number of
each sex was assembled, gave nine-tenths of its
area to the ladies, was just at that time about to
be introduced.

The ostensible pretext for her visit to London
was to put forward her claims to some property
bequeathed to her by a distant relation ; but in
reality she was an emissary in the pay of the
French Government, to whom was assigned the
task of assisting the manœuvres of the Jacobite
agents, and at the same time of reporting to
the French Ministers as to their activity, their
success, and (perhaps chiefly) their fidelity. It
was to suppress, as far as possible, all trace of
her connexion with the Parisian authorities
that she had been directed to make Genoa her
starting-place, and had obtained thence, through
the influence of Rome, introductory letters from
some Italian families of distinction.

Among the representatives of the Jacobite
cause to whom London had been assigned as
the scene of action, few were so able, so active,

or so influential as Martin Brerewood, and the relations between the Countess Molina and him had become proportionately confidential. Besides the political ties which knit them together, there existed a mutual admiration of each other's talents, a mutual liking for each other's society, and, it must be added, a mutual mistrust of each other's character. Her reticence as to her antecedents, which baffled all his ingenuity of research, her evidently false position in the social scale, her talent for political intrigue, her fertility of resource when difficulties occurred, her sagacity in discovering and taking advantage of the foibles of those with whom she came in contact, made it evident to Brerewood that, while she was a powerful ally, her position was too doubtful, and her abilities too versatile, to justify him in trusting her implicitly.

She, on the other hand, whilst she appreciated his personal attractions and accomplishments, as well as his rare energy and intelligence, quickly discerned the devouring ambition and intense selfishness which were his ruling passions, and to which every other feeling was unscrupulously sacrificed.

Mr. Brerewood was ushered into the boudoir of the countess, a small room cut off by a narrow passage from the principal apartments, and so isolated as to secure complete privacy. It was luxuriously appointed, and replete with those tasteful ornaments and elegant trifles which women take such delight in. The countess was seated at an escritoire, which on seeing her visitor she shut and locked, and rising welcomed him, saying in French, "Well, my preux chevalier, what success yesterday? Did you land the fish that you thought you had hooked? Sit down, and tell me about it."

So saying, and pointing to a chair, she seated herself on a low couch by its side.

"My dear countess," replied he, in the same language, for he spoke French fluently, "I found I had caught a snake instead of a fish, and I quickly threw him back into the water. I have every reason to believe that this seemingly obtuse person was set to catch me. We have tacitly agreed to ignore each other's existence. But what have you done with Lord Fernleigh?"

"After a few struggles," replied the countess, "he has yielded, and has shown me a letter of adhesion, indited by himself to His Majesty James III., which he is about sending by a sure hand to its address."

"Are you certain that it ever will be sent?"

"I shall only be certain when he assures me that it has been sent. His lordship's sense of honour makes nice distinctions. He will break a promise, but will not tell a lie. His pledges as to the future I place no reliance on, but his assertions as to the past I fully believe. What progress are you making with the Uppenhams?"

"I have their verbal and shall, in a day or two, obtain their written engagement," replied Brerewood, only telling half the truth.

"And their nephew, Mr. Allerton? You promised to introduce him to me. When will you bring him?"

"How insatiably curious you are, countess, about this pedantic puppy! You have cross-examined me twenty times about his appearance, his habits, and his morals, till I am sick of the subject; and now you want me to bring him here. What can be your motive?"

"Motive? As if a woman must always have a motive! Surely feminine curiosity is an all-

sufficient motive. However, you want a reason
for it? You shall have it. I want to see
young Allerton because—I want to see him;
and that is a true woman's reason. Will you
bring him?"

"I will, if you will engage to keep
him. I hate him : he is in my way where
he is.'

"Ah!" exclaimed the countess, sharply,
whilst she directed a keen glance at her visitor,
"you hate him? You want him out of your
way? What is your reason for this?"

"Reason?" replied Brerewood, with a touch
of sarcasm. "As if a man must necessarily
have reasons, any more than a woman!"

"My dear Mr. Brerewood, I am sure that
you have your reasons, and I think I can guess
them. They are not founded on political considerations, for you say you hate Mr. Allerton;
and you have no political hatreds. In that
sphere you rarely go beyond likes and dislikes.
You are actuated in this case by some strong
personal feeling. Surely—no, it cannot be
that—— Did you not tell me the other day
that Allerton was enamoured of his cousin, the
Uppenham girl?"

"Well, yes; what of that? I think I must leave you now; I have an appointment."

"And that she," continued the countess, without taking the slightest notice of his declared intention to depart, "seemed on very friendly terms with him. Yes, I see it all now; and it is charming! My dear Brerewood, I must congratulate you: you are in love."

"Absurd! But even supposing I were?"

"You are raised in my estimation, sir. Powerful intellect, lofty aims, indefatigable energy, I have always given you credit for; but I never was quite sure, till now, whether you had a heart. Love is a highly respectable weakness, and is, in your case, redeemed from commonplace by a smart infusion of jealousy."

"Really, madam, your banter is approaching the limits of my endurance. Do you take me for a tyro in love? Bah! 'I 've kissed and I 've prattled with fifty fair maids,' as the song says."

"I have no doubt of that; but, if I mistake not, this is your first serious affair. I can now understand how Mr. Allerton is in your way. Poor Mr. Brerewood! It is not so easy to displace, still less to replace, a favoured lover, especially as, living under the same roof, he and the Dulcinea are as constantly in each other's society as though they were married; perhaps a great deal more so.''

"Well, well! Admitting, just for the sake of the argument, that your surmise were correct, your observations are not very consoling."

"Consolations, my dear friend, are of very little use in such cases. What you want is assistance."

"If you could afford me the latter, I should be quite willing to dispense with the former."

The countess remained pensive a few minutes, while Brerewood, rising from his seat, paced impatiently up and down the room. At length she said,—

"Sit down, Mr. Brerewood, and listen to me. Supposing that I were able to assist you in a way you little dream of, and that, in order to do so, I decided on deviating from a course of action that I had long adopted and adhered to, what should I gain by such a sacrifice of a cherished scheme?"

"My dear countess," warmly exclaimed

Brerewood, "you would earn my eternal gratitude!"

"Of course, dear friend, that I should naturally expect. But what shape would that gratitude assume?"

"What shape?"

"Yes. You see, gratitude is so elastic a word: it may be the symbol of so many different things. It may mean a flow of elegant expressions, or a diamond ring, or the effectual furtherance of a favourite scheme, or an annuity for life; or it may remain a mere symbol never condensed into any practical result at all. Is it not so?"

"Ah, yes, I understand. But before we take a realistic view of that refined sentiment, gratitude, allow me to ask you what you propose to do for me. What would be the means that you would employ?"

"Before I answer, you must inform me what it is that you wish to be done."

"Of course, proceeding on the hypothesis you have so ingeniously framed, my first wish would be—"

"Hold, my friend! I cannot waste my time in devising and discussing schemes applicable to a supposititious case. Romances are charming to read, but I do not care contributing to the composition of one. Unless your love for Miss Uppenham and your jealousy of Mr. Allerton are realities, and admitted by you to be so, I must decline to interfere."

"Well, madam," said Brerewood, passionately, "have it so, if you will. I love Alice Uppenham ; I hate Francis Allerton. The one I intend to win for a wife ; the other I want to remove from that ' coign of 'vantage,' his uncle's house ; for while he is there he is in my way."

"As to winning the lady, you will hardly expect me to do that for you. So gallant a cavalier would never submit to the humiliation of making love by proxy. As to the removal of young Allerton from his uncle's roof, on what do you found your present hopes of success ? "

"The young fellow has a certain sturdy independence of mind; and entertaining, as he does, a strong tendency to Whig principles, there is a degree of political antagonism between him and the rest of the family which I am trying to work up into a feud. He has

been summoned to declare, in a few days,
'under which king' he intends to 'live or
die'; and as they are, all of them, an obstinate
set, especially the uncompromising aunt, I am
in hopes of creating a salutary amount of
discord and strife."

"Are you sure that a political would suffice
to ensure a domestic separation?"

"By no means sure; and that is just the point
at which I am most in want of assistance."

"But supposing young Allerton should
decide on siding with the cause which you and
I have so much at heart, and of which you have,
no doubt, in your conversations with him, been
so eloquent an advocate?"

"I have reason to believe that his decision
will be in a contrary direction. Indeed, to say
the truth, which, from your meaning smile, I
fancy that you guess at already, in my political
talk with Allerton I have been exceptionally
candid."

"Candid?"

"Yes; there is no deception like candour,
when it is properly directed. I have confessed
to him, what we carefully conceal from others,
and as much as we can from ourselves, the

ignoble motives — ambition, selfishness, and venality — which actuate three-fourths of the leaders of the Jacobite party in England."

"And no doubt you were equally candid in your exposition of His Sacred Majesty James III.'s views as to divine rights, passive obedience, &c. ?"

" I was ; but I tempered my admissions with regrets that so holy a cause should be open to such blemishes, and obliged to use such tools, with assurances that the evil was temporary and remediable, and with hopes that what I had, in a moment of impulsive frankness, incautiously disclosed would not prejudice him against our party. Above all, I appealed to him not to take advantage of my indiscretion, and easily persuaded him to promise entire secrecy."

" I admire your insidious artlessness ; but tell me, do you think that the uncle and aunt are favourable to Allerton's views towards their daughter ?"

" I have studied that question, but have not quite solved it. I incline to believe that, inasmuch as the young people were brought up together from childhood as brother and sister, the elders have not yet looked seriously at the contingency of their becoming anything else to each other. And now, fair lady, I have answered your questions, do you still see your way to promote my designs?"

"I do; but—"

"But my definition of eternal gratitude must be satisfactory?"

"I was not thinking of that just now; but, since you put me in mind of it, you may take it for granted that that is one condition."

"And will you now acquaint me with the nature and source of that mysterious influence which is to be so powerfully exerted on my behalf?"

"Far from that, I have not even made up my mind whether I shall use it or not."

"'Sdeath! madam, you do not mean to say that you have led me on by a false lure to make these revelations of my secret feelings and projects to gratify your idle curiosity, and to leave me, after all, in the lurch?"

"I promised nothing," said the countess, coldly.

"No; but you led me to expect much," replied Brerewood, warmly; "and you are mistaken if you fancy that I shall tamely sub-

mit to the indignity of having succumbed to
your wiles, and gratuitously unveiled to you
my innermost thoughts and aspirations."

"Calm yourself, Mr. Brerewood: your sus-
picions are unjust. The step which I am disposed to take in your favour involves such a
disturbance of my previous plans that I do not
choose to commit myself to it without further
reflection. Remember that it has suggested
itself in the course of this conversation, and it
is too important a measure for me to adopt on
the spur of the moment. I shall let you know
my decision."

"And when shall I be made acquainted with
it? There is no time to lose, and I detest
being kept in suspense."

"Listen to the way in which I propose to
deal with the matter. Arrange with Mr.
Allerton that you and he shall pay me a visit
on Saturday evening next. I shall be alone,
and prepared to take a decided course. Do
you think that you can induce him to
come?"

"Yes; I have little doubt of it. I have
excited in him some curiosity about you, and
he has signified his willingness to accompany

me on any evening that you might name to receive us."

"Good. Now to the second point. Mr. Brerewood, I want money. My remittances come irregularly from France, and my expenses are heavy. Are you prepared to meet me on this point?"

"Fully, countess. I naturally expected such a demand. But do not amerce me in too heavy a sum. Remember that what I have to get in return is at present an unknown quantity."

"I know that you will be hard of belief, but I assure you that money is the smallest of the considerations that induce me to contemplate interference in the affair, and indeed is merely the feather that turns the scale between two conflicting sets of motives."

"Very well, my dear countess, I will contribute the feather, and it shall help to warm your nest."

"Then bring with you a small packet that shall contain a fifty-pound bank-note, and a written engagement to pay me two more fifties when Mr. Allerton shall, in consequence of my procedure, be compelled to quit his uncle's roof."

"That seems reasonable, and not over expensive. Shall we then close the bargain?"

"Not yet. When you see me on Saturday evening you will offer me the packet as from a friend; let us call her Lady Jones. If I refuse it, saying that it is a mistake, you will conclude that, on deliberation, I have declined taking any part in the matter in question."

"Can you not let me know before then?"

"No; I will only decide then. But if I accept the packet, that will be a token that I agree, and I shall then proceed at once to the execution of my project."

"What, on the spot?—with only Allerton and myself present? Then you intend speaking to him about it? How can you possibly expect that he will listen to—Pshaw! it seems absurd."

"It is not my habit to deal in absurdities. Trust to me. Perform you your part; I shall be prepared to perform mine."

Having concluded this curious arrangement, Brerewood took his departure.

CHAPTER XIV.

A DISAGREEABLE SURPRISE.

WHEN Alice and I had returned home from our delicious walk on that blissful Saturday she ran upstairs to her room, no doubt to think it all over again; and I proceeded to the drawing-room, where I found my uncle and aunt apparently absorbed in serious conversation, which they abruptly suspended when they saw me approach.

"Frank," said my uncle, "I want a few words with you; but I will not detain you long, as I know that you have an appointment with Mr. Brerewood. I met him to-day, and he told me that he was to call for you this evening."

"Thank you, my dear uncle; but, if you want me, I would prefer to stay with you to going out. Indeed, I am somewhat fatigued with my walk, and would rather not accompany Mr. Brerewood."

" I think," said my aunt, " that it would be wrong to disappoint Mr. Brerewood, since he is coming purposely to fetch you."

" Yes, Frank, you had better go," said my uncle ; " but you can spare half an hour to resolve our doubts, once and for ever, as to the part you intend taking in the political struggle which is now fast approaching."

During the few days that had elapsed since my uncle had exacted from me a promise that I would, without delay, arrive at a decided opinion on the paramount political question of the day, and assume a definite position with regard to it, I had given the subject the most serious consideration. My leaning had always been towards the Protestant succession as now established ; and continued investigation and reflection had now converted that leaning into a conviction. Not that the present order of things was by any means perfect, but what it was proposed to substitute for it seemed to me worse ; and to purchase a deterioration at the price of a civil war looked to me very much like a criminal absurdity. I had therefore deter-

mined that I would not be a party to the sub-
version of the present form of government, and
the only sacrifice I could conscientiously make
to my uncle's views was a discreet and im-
partial neutrality. I therefore replied,—

" Is it absolutely necessary that I should
take a decided part in a conflict wherein
honesty of purpose and conscientious convictions animate so many true men on each side?"

" Fie! Frank," exclaimed my aunt. " There
may, as you say, be true men on each side; but
those are no true men who weakly palter
between one side and the other."

" My dear nephew," interposed my uncle,
" I have more than once urged upon you, and
you have more than once promised me, to institute a careful and solemn inquiry into the vital
question that divides by a fathomless gulf the
friends of royalty from the friends of revolution. Have you performed your promise?"

" I have, uncle, so far as my abilities go."

" And your verdict? Speak out, Frank; I
put it to your conscience as an honest man to
declare it unmistakably."

" Then on my conscience, uncle, I believe
that it would be adverse to the interests of the

country to subvert the existing Government."

"I thought so!" exclaimed my aunt. "Alas for the Allertons!"

"Stay, my dear," said my uncle. "While we lament his error, we cannot but applaud his truthfulness."

"My dear uncle and aunt, do not take it ill that I cannot share your political opinions, and, above all, do not imagine that I am so conceited as to sit in judgment upon them. I fully acknowledge that I am your inferior in capacity as well as in experience, and that your power of sifting right from wrong exceeds mine. But it was at your request that I undertook to investigate the subject and draw my own conclusions. If in seeking for truth I have lighted on what you deem a falsity, it is at least the result of conscientious inquiry, and it has become a sincere conviction."

"The more earnest your belief, Frank," said my aunt, with some severity of tone, "the more hopeless is your conversion. Meredith, it is in great measure your fault. Instead of instilling into his mind fixed and definite principles, you have encouraged in him a spirit of independent research, and you see where it has led ! "

" My dear," gravely responded my uncle, " principles which are not of native growth in the mind, but are only transplanted there ready grown, enjoy but a feeble vitality."

" A house divided against itself cannot stand," observed my aunt. " What is to be done ? "

This observation pointed to a possible change in the amicable relations that had always subsisted between us, and I was filled with alarm. But two or three hours before I had reached the summit of felicity by receiving from Alice the assurance that my love for her was returned ; and now, just as I was about asking from her parents their consent to our union, grave differences had arisen between us, on a subject to which I knew that they (and especially my aunt) attached the utmost importance.

" But, my dear aunt," said I, " pray do not talk of division. Do not let me be the slightest hindrance to the prosecution of your plans. All I seek for, what I would be grateful to you for allowing me, is simple neutrality."

" I do not believe in neutrality," rejoined my aunt. " I cannot conceive any person being neutral, that is to say, indifferent, heedless, and, so to say, colourless, in a matter like this, which is not merely an abstract theory, but a living principle, which must be actively fought for or fought against. He who is not with us is against us."

" I think," said my uncle, "that we had better not prolong the present discussion. Mr. Brerewood will be here directly; and while you are out, Frank, your aunt and I will think and talk over the matter."

I took the hint, for I was myself rather at a loss how to continue a conversation that had assumed so embarrassing a tone, and accordingly I went to my room to prepare myself for my visit at the house of the lady to whom Brerewood was to introduce me. He came shortly after, and, as the evening was fine, we agreed to walk to Clarges Street, where this lady resided.

" Do you expect," asked I, as we walked along, " that there will be much company at the countess's to-night ? "

" I fancy not," replied Brerewood; " Wed-

nesdays are her reception-days, not Saturdays.
Besides, as she has expressed rather a pressing
wish to make your personal acquaintance, I
suppose she will want to converse more with
you than she could do if her company were
numerous. Did you ever hear her name
before I casually mentioned it to you?"

" Never. What makes you ask?"

" Nothing; except that, from one or two
expressions that fell from her unwittingly, I
fancy that she has some knowledge of your
family."

" Not impossible : my father many years
ago lived a good deal in France. Is your
acquaintance with this Countess Molina of old
date?"

" By no means," replied Brerewood. " She
came from Genoa a few months ago, with letters
of introduction to first-rate people here. Some
of these were friends of mine, and through
them I formed her acquaintance. She is very
entertaining, clever, and rather caustic. She
exercises her wit on her foes even in their
presence, and, of course, on her friends when
they are absent."

" Then it may be better to be her foe than her

friend ; for the former, being present, may parry
her attacks, while the latter, being absent, is
defenceless."

"Yes ; but the blow dealt on your person
may hurt you, while that aimed at your
shadow is unfelt."

In such talk we beguiled the time till we
arrived at our destination. I must have proved,
however, but poor company, as my mind was
continually reverting to the contrast between
my delightful *tête-à-tête* with Alice and my
unpleasant interview, subsequently, with her
parents. I certainly was not in a frame of
mind to make a very favourable impression
on the new acquaintance I was about to
visit.

We found the Countess Molina alone ; not in
the great reception-room, but in a smaller one
beyond. She accorded me a gracious reception, and, after a short chat on trivial topics,
Brerewood went over to her and presented her
with a small packet, adding a few words which
I could not catch. She took it, saying,—

" Thanks ; I will see that it is carefully
acknowledged."

Then turning to me, she observed,—

"I believe you were born in France, Mr. Allerton, were you not?"

"I was, madam."

"Have you agreeable reminiscences of your native country?"

"Hardly any at all, agreeable or otherwise. My father brought me to England when a mere child, and I have never visited France since then."

"Have you any remembrance of the persons composing your father's household at the time you quitted Paris?"

"Really, my recollections of that period are very confused, and I have never cared much to recur to them."

"I hope, Mr. Allerton, that it will not be disagreeable to you to have the events of your early life recalled to your memory; for, to say the truth, that is the precise purpose for which I requested Mr. Brerewood to bring you here."

I was too amazed to reply at once to this speech, which struck me as bordering on impertinence, and which certainly was totally unexpected. I looked at Brerewood, and he at me. Astonishment was depicted on both our countenances; but in his there was a lurking smile, as though his surprise were mingled with a sense of amusement.

"Pray, Mr. Allerton," continued the countess, seeing that I did not answer, "do you remember a person of the name of Zillah?"

I did recollect such a name; but, piqued by this unwarrantable intrusion into my private affairs, I determined not to submit to her cross-examination.

"Madam," I replied, "do me the favour to select some other topic for conversation. I must frankly avow my distaste to that which you have just introduced."

"I am sorry, indeed, for that," rejoined the countess, "as I am compelled to pursue the theme, however unwelcome. Since you decline answering my questions, I will myself impart the information which they were intended to elicit."

"I cannot divine, madam, your motive for making these communications; but I do not think that any motive can justify you in making them against the will of the person whom they chiefly concern, and I decidedly object."

"Ah, you object, do you?" said the countess, rising abruptly, and speaking with some vehemence. "Do you dare assume a tone of defiance? Well, then, listen! This Zillah was your mother, and not, as the world has been imposed upon to believe, Madame Allerton. You are the illegitimate son of Andrew Allerton!"

At this terrible announcement I started to my feet, as did Brerewood.

"Mr. Brerewood," I warmly exclaimed, "have you knowingly brought me here to receive the insult implied by this infamous fabrication?"

"On my word," replied he, "I had not the faintest idea of the facts which—"

"Facts?"

"Well, of the allegations that have just been set forth by this lady."

"Pray acquit Mr. Brerewood of all knowledge of the secret that I have just divulged," said the countess, coolly.

I was paralyzed with astonishment at the unparalleled audacity of the statements so rudely made. While I was endeavouring to think of what I should say or do, I saw Brerewood go

up to the countess, and in an undertone, which
however was audible to me, he said to her,
"Are you not going too far?" She answered
him abruptly and loudly, "No!" He shrugged
his shoulders and retired. It was evident to me
that he no more believed her story than I did.

"Brerewood," I said at last, "it is clear that
something has disordered the brain of this lady.
Who is she that dares to utter such scandalous
falsehoods?"

"Who is she, you ask? Well, you shall
know," passionately exclaimed the countess.
"I am Zillah! I am your mother!"

"Phew!" said Brerewood, half to himself; "another tremendous clap of theatrical
thunder!"

As for myself, this new imposture added intense disgust to my indignation.

"Let us go," I said : "the woman is mad."

"Stay!" said the countess, in a fierce voice,
almost amounting to a shriek. "Have you the
audacity, Frederick,—for that is your name, and
not Francis,—to deny that you for years have
been aware of the facts I have just stated, for
years have been parading a false name, and
knowingly assuming a false position?"

"Woman!" I cried, boiling over with rage, "if you are not mad, you must be atrociously wicked to forge such lies."

"What!" said she, in a somewhat calmer tone, "do you mean seriously to assert that you had not till now become acquainted with the secret of your birth? But—bah! I am not to be deceived: you have known it for years!"

"Really, countess," expostulated Brerewood, "you are pressing Mr. Allerton too hard. Whatever amount of truth there may prove to be in the version you have given of his birth, of this I am quite certain (and I owe it to him to declare it), that it is new to him, and takes him by surprise as much as it does me."

By this time I had somewhat cooled down, and I began to see clearly that I could gain nothing by losing my temper, and that I had better treat the whole affair with contempt.

"Mr. Brerewood," I said, "I must decline holding any further communication with this person; but for your satisfaction, and in justice to myself, I must aver to you that I never till now heard a single syllable of the story we have just been told, and I entertain not the

some foundation of truth in this story? The bare possibility made me shudder. What? was I no longer Francis Allerton, the legitimate son, but Frederick Something, the offspring of this woman? This woman my mother? Horrible! I hated her. Was it all a dream? I determined to fly home and read the fatal packet that was to fix my destiny for ever.

These thoughts flashed like lightning through my mind, and, turning to the countess, I said—

" Madam, if you are really under the impression that you have spoken the truth, and are simply labouring under some hallucination, there may be an excuse for the pain that you have to-night inflicted on me. But if I discover that you have wantonly annoyed me by calumnious fabrications, my respect for your sex shall not save you from the effects of my just resentment."

" Young man," replied the countess, with a certain amount of scornful dignity, " before you assume this pompous style, go home and read the document which it was your duty to have read long ago, and you will then talk in a different strain."

I then left the room hastily, without bidding adieu even to Brerewood, and rushed out of the house. I began by walking at a rapid pace in the direction of home; but soon my legs tottered, a feeling of faintness overcame me, and I was compelled to lean against some railings to prevent myself from falling. This was the third time this day that my feelings had been excited to their highest pitch. The glowing hopes, the beaming joy, which my interview with dear, dear Alice had raised in my heart were now overshadowed by gloomy misgivings verging on the darkness of despair.

I had been for some minutes brooding over my altered prospects, and was recovering from the physical weakness that had temporarily prostrated me, when I heard a rapid footstep approaching, and in another moment Brerewood had taken hold of my arm, and we were walking leisurely together.

" Allerton," said he, " I was perfectly amazed and shocked at what fell from the lips of Countess Molina this evening. I trust that it will all prove a delusion of hers."

" I trust so—I think so," replied I, very much annoyed to have to hold any converse on the subject, "but do not let me detain you; it is getting late."

" Indeed I must accompany you home. You seem ill and shaky, and I cannot leave you so. You will, of course, sift this story thoroughly."

"Of course—of course. I can get on very well alone, thanks."

"No doubt you had strong motives for not opening the packet from your father when it was delivered to you?"

" I thought I was doing for the best; but why should I trouble you to accompany me any further ?"

"It is no trouble, and it is only what you would do to me under similar circumstances. Perhaps you did not care about reading the paper because you knew the contents from other sources ?"

"Indeed, not so; you do me injustice. If I had known any facts approaching in the remotest degree to the circumstances set forth to-night, do you think that—"

"Oh, of course. Pray forgive me; I did not think of that. The question escaped me unthinkingly."

"Really, Mr. Brerewood, I would rather that

you left me to walk home quietly, pondering on the singularity of my position."

" Your position, as you say, is a singular one; and if I can be of any assistance to you, pray command me. Do you think that Mr. Uppenham has not all along been aware of the contents of your father's paper?"

" It is a painful effort, Mr. Brerewood, to apply my mind to the subject for the present. Pray leave me," and I withdrew my arm from his.

Seeing me resolute, he said, " Good night," and went his way.

The moment I arrived home, I flew upstairs to my own room, took the packet from its hiding-place, and, tearing it open, read what follows.

CHAPTER XV.

I, ANDREW ALLERTON, was born in 1693, of a good old Berkshire family, whose residence was the Allerton Manor-house, in the village of the same name. Whether the village was named after the family, or the family after the village, was a question never determined, nor ever worth determining. What can it matter? My grandfather, who was one of Charles II.'s graceless favourites, brought a large accession of wealth (how obtained it is bootless to inquire) to the moderate patrimony which he had inherited; and as he had been a spendthrift in his youth, and had become grasping in his middle career, he by a natural progression slided into avarice in his old age.

My father Mathew found himself, one fine

day, deprived of an asthmatic and stingy parent, and possessed of an ample fortune. He affected deep regret for the former, and proceeded without delay to squander the latter. He was, like all our race (I know it to my cost), cursed with passions of almost uncontrollable intensity, and if he ever did try to check them (which may be doubted) he entirely failed; for they certainly had their full play. He married a cousin, one of the Broughtons; and as she was as proud, as imperious, and as obstinate as he was, they led a sad life. Wine, women, and the gaming-table soon undermined his strong constitution, and dissipated most of his ample fortune.

The children were four in number—three boys and a girl. I was the second born, Francis the eldest, Frederick the next in succession to me, and Jane, the girl, the youngest of all. Frederick, at nineteen, fell in love with the daughter of a wealthy tradesman, and, with the headlong impetuosity of his race, contracted a clandestine marriage with her; then, knowing that he would never be forgiven by his father, he emigrated suddenly with his bride to Virginia. Whether he was tomahawked by the

Indians, or became a wealthy planter, we never knew, as he was not heard of any more.

The storm of anger which this event excited in the head of the family was, as might have been expected, extravagant. He exhaled a portion of his fury in maledictions upon us, the children who had not absconded, and in biting sarcasms against the wife of his bosom, who had no more to do with it than he had. He then hastened to London to efface the excitement of wrath by that of gambling.

A few weeks afterwards my ill-fated father was killed in a midnight broil with the riotous and ferocious Mohawks—a convivial band composed of young fellows belonging to some of the noblest and wealthiest families in England. It appears that he was pursuing an intrigue with some citizen's wife, and having disguised himself in the dress of a tradesman, on his way home he was taken for one of that class by the howling, drunken Mohawks (they never selected any person of quality for their prey), and assailed accordingly. Not that they had any design upon his life or purse,—oh no; all they wanted was amusement, and what could be more amusing than to place their victim inside a large barrel, which they always had at hand, and then roll him along the streets, with hoarse pæans of victory to drown the cries of the sufferer ? This they attempted to do with my father, but they found in him a man of other mettle. He drew his sword and laid about him furiously, wounded several of the noble revellers, who, irritated at this unjustifiable resistance on the part of a low shopkeeper, pierced him through and through, and left him dead on the spot.

Needless to say that when the rank of the murdered man was recognized there was a loud outcry, and what would have been deemed a venial offence if a man of low degree had been the martyr was stigmatized as a shameful outrage. But how to discover the guilty parties ? There was no evidence to fix the crime on any one. A wealthy baronet, and the younger son of a duke, were strongly suspected to have been the ringleaders ; but the scent gradually grew cold, and very soon the pursuit was relinquished.

After the solemn mockery of a gorgeous funeral, my mother ascertained, by means of the family lawyer, that, although very serious inroads had been made in the patrimony my father had inherited, he had not had time to squander the whole, which was fortunate for us.

At the time of my father's death, in 1714, I was of age, and my brother Francis two years older. We were very fond of each other, though constantly quarrelling. Our mother doted on us both; but her imperious nature could not brook our wayward freaks nor bear with our outbursts of temper, so that days of sunshine alternated with days of stormy strife. Our family had never known any other atmosphere than that of discord; and self-will, self-indulgence, and impatience of control seemed to be the special attributes of our race. Soon a fresh calamity spread desolation amongst us. A virulent form of that curse to humanity, the small-pox, pervaded the village of Allerton. It reached the Manor-house, and all the family, as well as most of the servants, were smitten by the horrible infection. My mother and elder brother died of it. I escaped, after being despaired of; but I was furrowed all over with the unseemly scars that disfigure so many of the victims of this modern plague. My sister Jane fortunately recovered without incurring this terrible penalty, so much more intolerable to a woman than to us.

The loss of my mother and brother (especially that of the former) caused me unutterable grief. Not a week had passed, during her lifetime, without some fresh feud starting up between us. Bitter words were frequently exchanged. I inveighed against her as a tyrant; she reviled me as a rebel; and yet underlying these fierce contentions a vast fund of mutual fondness dwelt in both our hearts. I knew that she loved me devotedly; it was, perhaps, the love of the tigress for her whelps, but I revelled and reposed in it, and felt that, come what may, my mother and I would have stood side by side against the whole world.

Now I was left solitary and without a tie on earth except my sister Jane, with whom I had little sympathy. She was as proud and self-willed as the rest of us, but her manner was cold and undemonstrative. She had been promised in marriage, not without her consent, but certainly without any display on her part of rapturous love, to Mr. Uppenham, a young gentleman of good family and fair position.

He was one of those tiresome persons called respectable. His morality verged on Puritanism, his good-breeding on priggishness, and his learning on pedantry. He was painfully good, and I was not sorry when, a decent time having elapsed, the marriage took place, and he carried my sister off to his own home.

About this time (August, 1715) the Earl of Mar summoned the friends of King James to rally round him in Scotland, and he soon collected a considerable force. In Lancashire, too, the gallant Forster, aided by the Earl of Derwentwater, Viscount Kenmure, and many other noblemen and gentlemen, raised the standard of revolt against the Hanoverian sway, and determined to die or reinstate the Stuart dynasty on the throne, now wrongfully occupied by a German usurper. Our race had always been loyal to the core, and the opportunity thus afforded me of drawing my sword in the good old cause I embraced with avidity. I raised all the money I could by mortgage and loan, and with plenty of gold in my valise, two fine horses, and one faithful attendant, Antony, rode swiftly on to join Forster in the North. Antony was the son of our old steward, and a devoted adherent both of the house of Stuart and the house of Allerton. He divided his allegiance between them, and when both came to grief transferred it to Mr. Uppenham, who, to do him justice, was also a friend to the rightful cause, in his timid, respectable way.

I need not advert to our defeat. Lukewarmness, incapacity, treachery, and divided counsels made failure inevitable. At the battle of Preston I narrowly escaped being made prisoner, but got away with a gash across the face, which harmonized gracefully with the marks which the small-pox had not long before imprinted on it. Antony stuck to me, and together we got to Liverpool, whence, by means of an extortionate bribe, a passage to Havre was obtained, and thus we escaped the untoward fate which attended many of our brave and noble friends. By the time I arrived at Paris I had nearly expended all my money. King James had gone on his wild-goose chase to Scotland, where he arrived too late, and whence he departed too early. He landed at Peterhead on Christmas Day, just in time to find his cause lost, and re-embarked for France on the 10th of January, without making any attempt to renew the struggle.

At Paris I met with many friends (friends? well, yes, friends in a way) of my father, who had left behind him lively recollections of his eccentricities. It so happened that licentiousness had just come into fashion. The old king, Louis XIV., who had sinned as long as he could, and who, when he grew old, and could sin no more, became an austere devotee, had died a few days before; and the witty, dissolute, and good-natured regent, D'Orléans, inaugurated quite a new order of things. Just as free-and-easy Charles II. rescued mirth and pleasure and "their crew" from the stony grasp of strait-laced Cromwell, so in France the riotous revels of the Regency succeeded to the gloomy asceticism of Louis XIV.

I threw myself greedily into this vortex of dissipation, and was soon admitted to the delightful suppers of the Palais Royal. The regent distinguished me by his favour; and I even obtained the goodwill of a much more powerful man, his preceptor and minister, Abbé Dubois. This curious compound of the most opposite qualities was then rising rapidly to supreme power. A mere plebeian, he was hated and courted, despised and worshipped, by the proudest nobles in the land.

I had soon spent all the money I had brought with me, and having nearly exhausted all my borrowing power, one day, finding Dubois in exceptionally good humour, I ventured, in a fit of desperation, to tell him how I was situated. Fortunately—for he was generally cynical and morose—he took it in good part.

"Allerton," said he, "I like your audacity. There is not another man in France who would have selected the Abbé Dubois. for his father-confessor. Well, I must justify your foolhardy trust in me. Are you married?"

"No."

"Will you marry?"

"A woman, or a fortune?" boldly asked I.

"Both."

"Decidedly, yes; but the prettier the one, and the larger the other, the better!" replied I.

"Diable!" said he, "you are particular. But *j'ai votre affaire.* I am very intimate with the Countess of Feuillemorte. Now she"—

"Many thanks, Monsieur l'Abbé; but I would sooner cut off my right hand than"—

"Bah! you goose," interrupted Dubois, in his turn; "it is not her that I am proposing to you. I have not done with her yet. She has a niece maturing in a convent, just expanding into womanhood, of whose hand and fortune I can dispose. You shall have her."

"How can I have deserved so rich a boon?"

"Do not ascribe it," he replied, "altogether to my desire to assist you. I have private reasons for wishing this heiress to become the wife of a foreigner. The arrangement I propose will suit you and enter into my own views. So expect to receive a card of invitation to la Comtesse de Feuillemorte's Wednesday's reception, and I will see that Mademoiselle Henriette shall be present."

"But perhaps, sir," I humbly suggested, "I may not find favour in the lady's eyes."

"Bah!" said Dubois, "that would not matter. But you are too modest. Barring your face, which is awfully ugly, your voice, which is harsh, your temper, which is violent, and your circumstances, which are desperate, you are an excellent *parti* for any lady."

To cut the matter short, all was soon arranged. The countess, for reasons I could never divine,

seemed anxious for the match ; and as for Henriette, she in her shy, coy manner evinced no
repugnance to the husband thus provided for
her. She was very pretty, very graceful ; and
her manners, like her smile, were most winning.
She seemed to take much pleasure in listening
to my adventures in the North of England,
and I suppose that my ghastly features were,
like Othello's copper skin, atoned for by " the
dangers I had passed."

The marriage soon took place. Henriette's
fortune was settled upon her ; but a large sum
of money, the surplus of several years' revenue
over the expenditure, was handed to me.
In this way I was relieved from all my pecuniary difficulties. Surely now, if ever, I might
have been happy. My wife was all that a husband could wish—handsome, kind, affectionate,
thoughtful, and so sweet tempered that my
occasional paroxysms of anger or cynicism had
little apparent effect upon her. She waited
patiently till the storm had expended its fury,
forgot or overlooked the unjust and offensive
words that might have dropped from me in my
rage, and when she saw the right moment had
arrived, she would look at me fixedly, and with

a meaning smile say, "If I have done or said
aught amiss, dear Andrew, forgive me"; or on
some other occasion would cast her arms round
my neck, exclaiming in a mock-tragical tone,
"Soyons amis, Cinna," under which treatment
I speedily recovered, and clear, brilliant sunshine succeeded to the tempest.

I had sense enough to know how much
superior her patient love was to my fitful fondness. Often, when the reaction set in from such
outbreaks of temper, have I passionately sworn
to her that I would never again give way to
those insane ebullitions, and with tender
caresses have craved her forgiveness.

"Andrew, love," she would reply, "they are
in your very nature, and I accept them as part
of your dear self. You may curb, but can
hardly totally subdue them. But we will try
together, will we not?"

She was pure as falling snow, single minded,
truthful, and frank even to fearlessness. She
spontaneously told me that, before she had seen
me, her love had been sought by a young poet of
the name of D'Anglas, who had professed himself
deeply enamoured of her; that they had met at
the house of her aunt the comtesse, but never

alone; that he had plied her with odes, sonnets, songs, and lyric effusions of all kinds, as well as with prosaic and heroic letters; that she had sent him back the latter, but, on account of the real talent displayed in them, had retained the former, which, however, she now placed in my hands; that her sentiments towards this ardent lover had been confined to esteem for him personally, and her admiration had only extended to his productions, which were certainly very clever. This voluntary statement placed me quite at ease with regard to my wife's antecedents; for few women ever had so little to confess, and fewer still would have made any confession at all.

Again I say that surely now, if ever, I might have been happy. Far from it; for, whilst really feeling the warmest affection and the most tender regard for my admirable wife, I was acting towards her with the grossest deceit.

END OF VOL. I.

LONDON :
PRINTED BY E. J. FRANCIS AND CO.,
TOOK'S COURT AND WINE OFFICE COURT, E.C.

www.ingramcontent.com/pod-product-compliance
Lightning Source LLC
Chambersburg PA
CBHW031422020726
47499CB00005B/1547